the
ultimate
film
guides

Psycho

Director
Alfred Hitchcock

Note by Amanda Sheahan Wells

Longman

York Press

York Press
322 Old Brompton Road, London SW5 9JH

Pearson Education Limited
Edinburgh Gate, Harlow, Essex CM20 2JE, United Kingdom
Associated companies, branches and representatives throughout
the world

First published 2001
Second impression 2002

ISBN 0-582-43191-3

Designed by Vicki Pacey
Phototypeset by Gem Graphics, Trenance, Mawgan Porth, Cornwall
Colour reproduction and film output by Spectrum Colour
Produced by Pearson Education North Asia Limited, Hong Kong

contents

dedication For Daniel.

Psycho, more than any of my other pictures, is a film that belongs to film-makers, to you and me.

Alfred Hitchcock

———— /// ————

author of this note Amanda Sheahan Wells has a BA Hons in Film Studies & Drama from the University of Kent and an MA in Film & Television Studies from Westminster University. She taught film studies to A Level and undergraduate students at South East Essex College for seven years and now works as a journalist. She is also the author of the York Film Note on *A bout de souffle*.

background

trailer

Psycho is one of the key works of our age.

Robin Wood, Hitchcock's Films Revisited, 1989, p. 150

Memory, notorious liar that it is, led me to believe that *Psycho* was a fairly ordinary film enlivened by three delicious moments of horror. Quite wrong, of course. In fact it's one of Alfred Hitchcock's best, fascinating all the way through. (...) Even on second viewing the moments of horror lose none of their impact.

Barry Norman, The Daily Mail, 8 August 1969

I don't know if a contemporary audience can understand how terrifying the film was to our generation. No mainstream film had dealt with violence so directly. (...) At the time I thought it was a shabby little shocker that I enjoyed enormously, but it's extraordinary how after all these years it haunts you because of the power of Bates. (...) Once you've seen Norman Bates you have to live with him for ever, and that is a heavy burden.

Howard Schuman, The Guardian, 17 July 1998

As source of iconography and a virtuoso display of manipulative moviemaking, *Psycho* is – for better and worse – one of the most influential pictures ever made.

Philip French, The Observer, 2 August 1998

Throughout the Sixties and Seventies *Psycho* was regarded by critics as a sensationalist slasher movie. (...) Even when [Hitchcock] started to be regarded as an artist, *Psycho* was still

'every frame is magnificent'

> looked down on. In recent years it has become a highly venerated work. Every frame is magnificent and it is considered probably the most influential film made after Welles' *Citizen Kane*.
>
> Nick James, The Independent, 6 August 1999

reading psycho

Psycho is one of the most famous films in the history of the cinema. Norman Bates, the shower scene and the screeching violins of composer Bernard Herrmann's music score have all entered the collective cultural psyche of those living in the Western world.

The influence of the film is irrefutable. It has spawned a host of cinematic clichés, imitations, sequels, a shot-by-shot remake, a song and even an installation at a London art gallery. *Psycho* is also credited with creating a **genre** of its own – the slasher horror – with descendants ranging from *Dressed to Kill* (1980) to *A Nightmare on Elm Street* (1984).

A generation of modern film-makers, including Steven Spielberg, Martin Scorsese, Francis Ford Coppola, Oliver Stone and Brian De Palma, who were all in their teens or early twenties when *Psycho* was released in 1960, were undoubtedly influenced by the impact of *Psycho* on audiences and by Alfred Hitchcock's explorations of what he called 'pure film'. 'Dealing with Hitchcock is like dealing with Bach – he wrote every tune that was ever done. Hitchcock thought up practically every cinematic idea that has been used and probably will be used in this form,' said Brian De Palma (quoted in Rebello, 1998, p. 192).

the impact of psycho

Perhaps some of *Psycho*'s success and influence can be attributed to the fact that when Alfred Hitchcock unleashed his film on to the general public he challenged many of the conventions of Hollywood film-making and cinema-going prevalent at the time. In an unprecedented move Alfred Hitchcock sent out a dictum to all cinemas stating, 'The manager of this theatre playing *Psycho* has been instructed, at the risk of his life, not to admit any persons after the picture starts' (Paramount publicity

The publicity campaign
for *Psycho* warned audiences
that the film was going to be
bold and different

information). This was unheard of in 1960, when cinemas usually played main features, **B–movies** and shorts in a loop and people wandered in and out of the cinema whenever they felt like it. People would often come in midway through a film and then sit through everything until they got back to the point where they had started.

Alfred Hitchcock so wanted to engineer people's experience of *Psycho* he even put together a handbook for **exhibitors**. Entitled, 'The Care and Handling of *Psycho*', it outlined how to manage audiences and the screening of the film:

> Experience in all our opening engagements has shown us that it enhances the dignity and importance of *Psycho* to close your house curtains over the screen after the end-titles of the picture, and keep the theater dark for ½ minute. During these 30 seconds of stygian blackness, the suspense of *Psycho* is indelibly engraved in the mind of the audience, later to be discussed among gaping friends and relations. You will then bring up house lights of a greenish hue, and shine spotlights of this ominous hue across the faces of your departing patrons. Never, never, never will I permit *Psycho* to be followed immediately by a short subject or newsreel.
>
> *Rebello, 1998, p. 151*

Not only was the cinema-going experience of *Psycho* different, audiences were also confronted with a film that broke many cultural taboos and challenged the censors of the day at a time when social attitudes were shifting. As America and Europe moved away from the post-war austerity of the 1950s to the prosperity and decadence of the swinging 1960s, Alfred Hitchcock provided a number of shocking images: Janet Leigh in a brassiere just after she has made love to boyfriend Sam at the start of the film; Janet Leigh stabbed to death naked in the shower; Norman Bates as a cross-dressing psychopath and the first ever flushing toilet shown on screen.

But audiences were not only shocked by the content of *Psycho*. They were also reacting to a very new type of film. By the end of the 1950s

a roller coaster of shocks, surprise and suspense

Hollywood cinema was under threat from the growth in popularity of television, and audience figures were in decline. With *Psycho*, Alfred Hitchcock made a film that was different not only from what he had done before, but also from most of the Hollywood films that had gone before it.

During the period from the late 1920s to the late 1950s, Hollywood films were produced in a style referred to as **Classical Hollywood Narrative** (see Narrative & Form: Classical Hollywood Narrative). The Classical Hollywood Narrative style generally revolved around story and **stars**, and was usually heavy with dialogue. *Psycho* offered audiences a cinematic experience that was much more emotional and visceral. Spectators were caught up in a roller coaster of shocks, surprise and suspense based on image, editing and sound. Alfred Hitchcock had turned movie-going into an event – not only one where you had to arrive on time, but also one where the film had a very direct, emotional impact.

In an interview with François Truffaut, Alfred Hitchcock said:

> My main satisfaction is that the film had an effect on the audiences, and I consider that very important. I don't care about the subject matter; I don't care about the acting; but I do care about the pieces of film and the photography and the soundtrack and all of the technical ingredients that made the audience scream. I feel it's tremendously satisfying for us to be able to use the cinematic art to achieve something of a mass emotion. And with *Psycho* we most definitely achieved this. It wasn't a message that stirred the audiences, nor was it a great performance or their enjoyment of the novel. They were aroused by pure film.
>
> *Truffaut, 1985, pp. 282–3*

It is not implausible to trace many of the techniques of modern Hollywood cinema back to what Alfred Hitchcock achieved with *Psycho*. Now that television is the medium that best supplies us with talking heads, the modern blockbuster makes the most of the big screen to provide action and special effects sequences that will have a direct

the impact of psycho background

'a sad prostitution of a fine talent!'

impact on the emotions of its international audience. Modern blockbusters also rely on well-engineered publicity campaigns to turn the release of a film into an event that cannot be missed.

For all of the reasons given above it is clear that *Psycho* has had an indelible effect on the cinema. Yet when it was first released it was generally reviled by critics.

> I have just seen one of the most vile and disgusting films ever made. It is entitled *Psycho* and is showing at the de Mille Theatre on Broadway. The shocking thing is not only its repulsive contents, but the fact that it was made by, of all people, Alfred Hitchcock. (...) Now look here, Maestro Hitchcock, just what is the game? (...) Oh yes – of course, *Psycho* is brilliantly directed. But what a sad prostitution of a fine talent!
>
> Rene MacColl, Daily Express, 2 July 1960

> 'Who does he think he is!' Caroline Lejeune [film critic] repeated, as we left, shaken and shocked – and she promptly handed in her resignation from the *Observer*. If that's the way films were going, she wanted none of it. Hitch must have laughed darkly: not often you kill a critic, too.
>
> Alexander Walker, remembering the first time he saw Psycho,
> The Evening Standard, 30 July 1998

Alfred Hitchcock had certainly provoked the wrath of critics, even before they had seen the film. As Janet Leigh remembers,

> Critics, who were used to VIP treatment from all the **studios** in all parts of the world, rebelled at the handling they received from Mr. Hitchcock. He did not allow exhibitors anywhere to have private screenings for reviewers. (This was in line with his 'see it from the beginning' and secrecy platform. They might have given away the plot.) Instead they had to see the film with the regular paying public (...) and sit through the shorts and coming attractions.
>
> Leigh and Nickens, 1995, p. 105

Psycho was ahead of its time

However, it was not just their anger at Alfred Hitchcock's manipulative promotion methods, nor their possible unease at the film's exploration of **voyeurism** (see Narrative & Form: Narrative Structure and Hitchcock as Auteur) – which some commentators have suggested was perhaps a little unsettling for those whose vocation lay in watching – that led critics to reject *Psycho* at the time of its release. Like most great works of art, *Psycho* was ahead of its time.

In later years *Psycho* has gone on to be revered as one of the classics of cinema. In 1977 *Psycho* was selected by the American Film Institute as one of the fifty best American movies of all time. On the American Film Institute's '100 years, 100 movies' website, *Psycho* is placed at number eighteen in the centenary list of America's hundred greatest movies. And in 1999 a panel of experts voted *Psycho* as Alfred Hitchcock's best movie in a poll organised by the British film magazine *Sight and Sound*.

the production of psycho

So how did such a controversial, successful, influential film make it to the big screen? In the summer of 1959 a book by novelist Robert Bloch entitled *Psycho* was published. It was based on the true story of serial killer Ed Gein, an eccentric recluse who kept the remains of his murdered victims in his rambling farmhouse.

Prior to publication, Bloch's agent sent advance copies of his text to the Hollywood film studios. One reader at Paramount had this to say about the book:

> Too repulsive for films, and rather shocking even to a hardened reader. It is original, no doubt about that, and the author practices clever deceptions upon the reader, not revealing until the end that the villain's mother is actually a stuffed corpse. Cleverly plotted, quite scary toward the end, and actually fairly believable. But impossible for films.

Rebello, 1998, p. 13

production of psycho background

a budget of $800,000

One person in Hollywood, however, was interested, and Alfred Hitchcock bought the film rights to *Psycho*.

> I think that the thing that appealed to me and made me decide to do the picture was the suddenness of the murder in the shower, coming, as it were, out of the blue.
>
> *Truffaut, 1985, p. 268–9*

Alfred Hitchcock had just finished making the big-budget action thriller *North by Northwest* (1959) with Cary Grant and he was looking for his next project. He was reportedly interested in the low-budget horror films made by studios like Universal-International and Hammer Horror that were popular with the public, and set himself the challenge of making something similar, but in his own inimitable style.

Paramount, the studio where Alfred Hitchcock was working at the time, did not like *Psycho* and refused to finance it. Undeterred, he decided to go ahead with the project. He used his own production company, Shamley Productions, to finance the film, planned the film on a low budget without big stars, decided to use most of the crew from his television series *Alfred Hitchcock Presents* and secured a deal with Universal-International to film on one of its sound stages. Paramount agreed to **distribute** the film and as sole producer Alfred Hitchcock deferred his director's fee in exchange for sixty per cent ownership of the film's negative. This turned out to be one of Alfred Hitchcock's most lucrative decisions.

Psycho had a budget of $800,000 and a 36-day shooting schedule. Principal photography on production number 9401 began on 30 November 1959. The film was code-named Wimpey during production and filmed on a closed set. Actors and crew had to agree not to discuss the film with anyone and production photographs were carefully controlled. Alfred Hitchcock was determined to maintain complete secrecy about the film. Principal photography wrapped after two months on 1 February 1960, nine days over schedule.

When *Psycho* opened in the US in June 1960 no one was prepared for the effect it would have on audiences.

'Faintings. Walk-outs. Repeat visits. Boycotts'

No amount of optimism or carefully orchestrated hucksterism could have prepared anyone – least of all Alfred Hitchcock – for the firestorm the film was creating. Certainly no one could have predicted how powerfully *Psycho* tapped into the American subconscious. Faintings. Walk-outs. Repeat visits. Boycotts. Angry phone calls and letters. Talk of banning the film rang from church pulpits and psychiatrists' offices. Never before had any director so worked the emotions of the audience like stops on an organ console. Only the American public first knew what a monster Hitchcock had spawned.

Rebello, 1998, p. 162

Psycho went on to storm through Europe and South America during September and October of 1960. By the end of the first year of its release it had made $15 million at the box office – at a time when the average cost of a ticket was considerably less than a dollar. It has since gone on to gross well in excess of $40 million according to figures given in *Empire* in August 1998 (no. 110), and is placed at number 100 in the list of top grossing films ever, adjusted for inflation, on the movie times website (www.the-movie-times.com).

After the initial critical condemnation of the film, *Psycho* did receive a handful of Oscar nominations in spring 1961. Alfred Hitchcock was nominated for Best Director; Janet Leigh for Best Supporting Actress; John Russell for Cinematography and Robert Clatworthy and Joseph Hurley for Art Direction. However, *Psycho* left the Academy Awards ceremony without a single Oscar. Alfred Hitchcock had once again been ignored by the Academy.

biographies: cast

ANTHONY PERKINS

Psycho changed the lives of many of the people who worked on it, not least Anthony Perkins who could never really escape the character of Norman Bates in the public perception. Anthony Perkins was born in New York city in April 1932. He was the son of the Broadway actor Osgood

biographies: cast background

a tender, vulnerable young man

Perkins, who died when Anthony was five years old. Anthony Perkins wanted to be an actor from a young age and he appeared with theatre companies throughout his school holidays. He finally made his professional debut on Broadway in *Tea and Sympathy* (1954–5) and then moved on to television work. Anthony Perkins made his Hollywood debut in *The Actress* in 1953 and then took the starring role in *Fear Strikes Out* in 1957. He appeared in a number of other films in the late 1950s before being selected to play the part of Norman Bates. '"How would you feel if Norman were played by Anthony Perkins?" [Joseph Stefano recalled Hitchcock asking]. I said, "Now you're talking." I suddenly saw a tender, vulnerable young man you could feel incredibly sorry for' (Rebello, 1998, p. 39).

Anthony Perkins had a long career as an actor, working in Hollywood, Britain and France. However, he never could shake off the ghost of Norman. Eventually he reprised the role of Bates in the sequel *Psycho II* (1983), went on to direct *Psycho III* (1986) and appeared in *Psycho IV: The Beginning* (1990). Anthony Perkins reportedly had a relationship with a male matinee idol at the start of his career, but this was kept under wraps by the studios, which carefully managed the private lives of all stars. Anthony Perkins married photographer Berry Berenson in August 1973 and they had two sons. He died on 12 September 1992 of an AIDS-related illness.

JANET LEIGH

Anthony Perkins' co-star in *Psycho* was Janet Leigh. She was a bigger star than the young Anthony Perkins and caused quite a stir by being cast in such an unconventional role. Janet Leigh was 'discovered' in 1947 by film star Norma Shearer. The story goes that Janet Leigh's parents were running a ski lodge in Northern California. Her father propped a picture of the young Janet up on the reservations desk, which was spotted by Norma Shearer, on holiday at the resort, and taken back to MGM. Janet Leigh was signed to MGM on a stock contract for seven years – which was the norm in the days of the **studio system**. She made her debut in *The Romance of Rosy Ridge* (1947) and then went on to appear in many films during the late 1940s and 1950s. Janet Leigh reached the peak of her career between 1958 and 1962 when she starred in three of Hollywood's most controversial films of the period; first in Orson Welles's *Touch of Evil* (1958) then in *Psycho*, and finally in John Frankenheimer's *The Manchurian Candidate* (1962). She was also one of Hollywood's high profile stars at this time, married to Tony Curtis from 1951 to 1962. (Their daughter is Jamie Lee Curtis.)

Janet Leigh was ideal for the part of Marion Crane in *Psycho*. She recalled:

> He [Hitchcock] wanted a name actress because of the shock value, but he also wanted someone who could actually *look* like she came from Phoenix. I mean, Lana Turner might *not* be able to look like someone from there. He wanted a vulnerability, a softness.

> *Rebello, 1998, p. 61*

Janet Leigh never worked with Alfred Hitchcock again because, the director said, of the impact Marion Crane had had on the public. However, she has taken part in a number of discussions and documentary programmes about Alfred Hitchcock and written a book with Christopher Nickens entitled *Psycho: Behind the Scenes of the Classic Thriller*.

VERA MILES

For the other female lead in *Psycho*, the part of Marion Crane's sister Lila, Alfred Hitchcock cast Vera Miles. She was one of his protégés. He had spotted her in the 1950s television show *Medic* and then cast her in his *Alfred Hitchcock Presents* episode *Revenge* (1955). Vera Miles appeared in John Ford's classic film *The Searchers* (1956) and then signed a five-year personal contract with Alfred Hitchcock to star in three films a year. She starred in *The Wrong Man* (1956) and was due to star in *Vertigo* (1958) until she announced she was pregnant. The relationship between her and Alfred Hitchcock reportedly cooled after this. She didn't appear in any more of Alfred Hitchcock's films after *Psycho*, although she did appear in one more of his TV shows, *Incident at a Corner* (1960). She continued

Anthony Perkins, Vera Miles
and John Gavin led the cast of
Psycho after its star, Janet Leigh,
was murdered in the first half
of the film

collaborators from previous feature films

working as an actress in films and television, appearing in John Ford's acclaimed *The Man Who Shot Liberty Valance* (1962). She also reprised the role of Lila in *Psycho II*.

JOHN GAVIN

The character of Sam Loomis in *Psycho* was played by contract player John Gavin. He was fairly inexperienced at the time of shooting and appreciated Alfred Hitchcock's help on set.

> I was relatively new and only beginning to get the hang of it [acting] (...) So I liked the fact that Mr. Hitchcock said, 'At this point, we will have you in a full shot. And as you move here, it will be a waist shot.'
>
> Leigh and Nickens, 1995, p. 52

John Gavin continued acting throughout the 1960s and 1970s in films such as *Spartacus* (1960) and *Thoroughly Modern Millie* (1967). He went on to become the US Ambassador to Mexico during the Reagan administration in the 1980s.

biographies: crew

Owing to budgetary restraints and the need to shoot *Psycho* quickly, Alfred Hitchcock decided to employ some of the crew of his television programme *Alfred Hitchcock Presents*, as they were used to working to tight schedules. Two of the television crew given senior roles in *Psycho*'s production were Hilton Green, who was made assistant director, and John L. Russell who took charge of **cinematography**.

However, Alfred Hitchcock also called on the talents of some of his collaborators from previous feature films. Editor George Tomasini, who had worked with Hitchcock on *To Catch a Thief* (1955), *The Wrong Man*, *Vertigo* and *North by Northwest* was brought in to handle the editing demands of sequences such as the shower murder. Graphic designer Saul Bass was asked to work on the film's titles and **storyboards,** and respected composer Bernard Herrmann was given the task of creating the music for the film. Alfred Hitchcock liked to work with people whom he knew well and trusted. However, a newcomer to the Hitchcock stable, Joseph Stefano, was contracted to write the script.

JOSEPH STEFANO

The first person brought in to work on the **screenplay** of *Psycho* was James P. Cavanagh. However, Alfred Hitchcock did not like James P. Cavanagh's screenplay and so he was paid off and released. Joseph Stefano, a thirty-eight-year-old former songwriter who had recently taken up writing for television was then brought in. Once Alfred Hitchcock was finally convinced that Joseph Stefano could do the job he hired him on a week-by-week contract. Before Stefano went away and wrote the script, Alfred Hitchcock and Joseph Stefano held five weeks of daily story conferences to thrash out how *Psycho* could be transferred to the screen.

After the success of *Psycho*, Alfred Hitchcock was keen to work with Joseph Stefano again. He offered him the screenplay of *The Birds* (1963) but Joseph Stefano declined. Alfred Hitchcock then asked him to work on the screenplay for *Marnie* (1964), which he had planned as a star vehicle for Grace Kelly. In the end Grace Kelly couldn't do *Marnie*, and by the time Alfred Hitchcock was ready to do the film with Tippi Hedren, Joseph Stefano was involved with the 1960s TV science fiction series *The Outer Limits*, so they never did work together again. In 1990 Joseph Stefano wrote the screenplay for *Psycho IV: The Beginning*.

SAUL BASS

Saul Bass was one of the leading title designers working in Hollywood when Alfred Hitchcock contracted him to design the titles for *Psycho*. Saul Bass began his film career working on Otto Preminger's *Carmen Jones* (1954) and then designed titles for *The Man with the Golden Arm* (1955) and *The Seven Year Itch* (1955) before joining Alfred Hitchcock to work on *Vertigo* and *North by Northwest*. Writing about Saul Bass in *Sight & Sound* in April 1997, Pat Kirkham said, 'Bass pioneered a new type of title sequence, a mood-setting opening that acts much as a musical overture might.' And in the same article Martin Scorsese is quoted as saying:

'*Nobody* directs Mr. Hitchcock's pictures but Mr. Hitchcock'

> Saul Bass can convey the sense of an entire film in a short, very powerful and rigorous unfolding of images ... His best sequences pierce deep into the soul of the films they are introducing. They crystallise. They are poetry and at the same time they preserve the mysteries.

Saul Bass produced the titles for three of Martin Scorsese's films: *Cape Fear* (1991), *The Age of Innocence* (1993) and *Casino* (1995).

When Alfred Hitchcock contracted Saul Bass for *Psycho*'s titles he also made him 'pictorial consultant' and asked him to storyboard the film. This arrangement led to some controversy as Saul Bass has claimed that he in fact directed the shower sequence and the murder of Arbogast. While Saul Bass certainly stood in for Alfred Hitchcock during the filming of Arbogast's murder owing to Alfred Hitchcock's ill health that day, Alfred Hitchcock had to re-shoot and re-edit the footage to create the effect that he actually wanted. (Alfred Hitchcock believed that Saul Bass's version of events made Arbogast look too menacing.) However, many of those connected with the film, including screenwriter Joseph Stefano, deny that Saul Bass filmed the shower sequence. Janet Leigh said:

> Saul Bass was there for the shooting, but he never directed me. Absolutely not. Saul Bass is brilliant, but he couldn't have done the drawings had Mr. Hitchcock not discussed with him what he wanted to get. And you couldn't have filmed the drawings.
>
> Rebello, 1998, p. 109

'I was on that set every second. *Nobody* directs Mr. Hitchcock's pictures but Mr. Hitchcock,' said script supervisor Marshal Schlom (Rebello, 1998, p. 108).

BERNARD HERRMANN

Bernard Herrmann is credited with creating some of the best and most original film scores in the history of cinema. He started his professional career composing music for a ballet number in a Broadway musical and then went on to form the New Chamber Orchestra. His work for the

'the master of suspense'

Columbia Broadcasting System, writing background music for radio shows and conducting on air, brought him into contact with the young Orson Welles – who was producing radio plays with his Mercury Playhouse Theatre. Bernard Herrmann composed the music for Orson Welles's first film *Citizen Kane* (1941) and then *The Magnificent Ambersons* (1942). In the mid 1950s he started a long and fruitful collaboration with Alfred Hitchcock. Bernard Herrmann wrote the musical scores for Alfred Hitchcock's *The Man Who Knew Too Much* (1956), *The Trouble with Harry* (1955), *The Wrong Man, Vertigo, North by Northwest, Psycho, The Birds* and *Marnie.* The partnership came to an end when Alfred Hitchcock rejected Bernard Herrmann's score for *Torn Curtain* (1966), apparently under pressure from the studio to use a more contemporary soundtrack. Bernard Herrmann's other notable film scores include *Hangover Square* (1945), *The Day the Earth Stood Still* (1951), *Tender is the Night* (1962), the original *Cape Fear* (1962), *Jason and the Argonauts* (1963) and *Taxi Driver* (1976), which was released just after Bernard Herrmann died.

ALFRED HITCHCOCK

> In the history of the cinema, Alfred Hitchcock holds a unique position: he is the only director (...) whose name conjures up a specific image in the average filmgoer's mind (...) Today, he is the only director whose movies are sold on his name alone.
>
> Bogdanovich, 1963, p. 3

Alfred Hitchcock, 'the master of suspense', was born in Leytonstone, England on 13 August 1899. His father was a grocer and his family was Catholic. He attended a convent primary school briefly, followed by a boarding school and then St Ignatius College, run by the Jesuits.

A much-repeated story from Alfred Hitchcock's childhood is that his father sent him down to the local police station, when he was five or six years old, with a note asking for him to be locked up for a short time as punishment for some minor misdemeanour. Alfred Hitchcock himself has linked this incident to his lifelong fear of authority and the themes of guilt and wrongful accusations that so often surface in his films.

biographies: crew

Alfred Hitchcock left school at fourteen and enrolled at the School of Engineering and Navigation. His first job was as a technical clerk at an electric cable manufacturers in London. Alfred Hitchcock was a keen theatre- and cinema-goer and from an early age he demonstrated an artistic side. He enrolled part time on an art course at London University to learn drawing and eventually had his interests recognised at work where he was promoted to the advertising department to produce copy and graphic illustrations for newspaper advertisements and brochures.

Alfred Hitchcock was an avid reader of the film trade press, and in 1919 he discovered that Famous Players-Lasky, a Hollywood film company, was going to open a studio in London. The ingenious Alfred Hitchcock did some research into the properties it was planning to film, produced some appropriate title card sketches and took these along to the studio. Alfred Hitchcock started doing some part-time work on titles for Famous Players-Lasky, and eventually they offered him a full-time job.

As this was during the early days of cinema, Alfred Hitchcock was able to get involved in various aspects of film-making and he tried his hand at scriptwriting, art direction and as assistant director. He even had a go at directing in 1922, with the unfinished *Number Thirteen*. By now Alfred Hitchcock was working for Michael Balcon's Gainsborough studio and he was sent to Germany to work on a co-production with the famous UFA studio. Here Alfred Hitchcock was exposed to the influence of **German Expressionism**, which was flourishing in Germany in the early 1920s, and to the work of great silent directors such as F.W. Murnau, who was shooting *The Last Laugh* (1924) in the studio where Alfred Hitchcock was working.

Alfred Hitchcock directed his first full film *The Pleasure Garden* in 1925 and followed this with *The Mountain Eagle* in 1926. However, it wasn't until *The Lodger* received critical and popular acclaim in late 1926 that Alfred Hitchcock truly began to establish himself. Indeed, Alfred Hitchcock claims that *The Lodger* was, 'the first true Hitchcock movie' (Taylor, 1996, p. 75).

In December 1926 Alfred Hitchcock married editor Alma Reville, who he had worked with at Michael Balcon's studio since 1923. They stayed married until Alfred Hitchcock's death in 1980 and had one daughter, Patricia, in 1928. (Patricia appears in *Psycho* as Marion's colleague at the office.) Alma was an important guiding force throughout Alfred Hitchcock's directorial career, often working in the background on each Hitchcock project.

After the success of *The Lodger*, Alfred Hitchcock became the star of British cinema, producing hits such as *Blackmail* (the first British talking picture) in 1929, *The Man Who Knew Too Much* (1934), *The 39 Steps* (1935), *Sabotage* (1936) and *The Lady Vanishes* (1938).

With a strong reputation, Alfred Hitchcock was finally lured to Hollywood by independent producer David O. Selznick in 1939, just as war broke out in Europe. Alfred Hitchcock's first film in America was the Oscar-winning *Rebecca* (1940) and he seemed to adapt to the Hollywood way of working quite easily.

> Though his methods of making a film in advance on paper were peculiar by Hollywood standards, they could be quite readily accommodated to the Hollywood system. The secret was that they evidently worked, and anyone in Hollywood would go along with that. He, for his part, was immensely impressed by the sheer efficiency of the Hollywood studio machine.
>
> *Taylor, 1996, p. 159*

Throughout the 1940s Alfred Hitchcock was loaned out to a number of different studios, including RKO, Universal and 20th Century Fox, by the independent David O. Selznick. Alfred Hitchcock directed some very successful films in this period, including *Suspicion* (1941), *Shadow of a Doubt* (1943), *Spellbound* (1945) and *Notorious* (1946), but there were also films that were less successful, such as *Mr and Mrs Smith* (1941) and *The Paradine Case* (1947). For a brief period at the end of the 1940s Alfred Hitchcock set up his own production company, Transatlantic Pictures, with his producer friend Sidney Bernstein. They produced two films, the successful *Rope* (1948) and the less successful *Under Capricorn* (1949), which led to the liquidation of the company. After this, Alfred Hitchcock returned to the fold of the Hollywood studios, with a contract at Warner Brothers, where he made four films. *Stage Fright* (1950), *Strangers on a Train* (1951), *I Confess* (1953) and *Dial M for Murder* (1954).

In 1953 Alfred Hitchcock moved to Paramount on a much more advantageous contract, 'one which gave him almost complete freedom and even guaranteed him that the later films he was to make for them would revert completely to his ownership after a period of eight years from the Paramount release' (Taylor, 1996, p. 222). While at Paramount, Alfred Hitchcock reached what many consider to be the peak of his career with films like *Rear Window* (1954), *To Catch a Thief* (1955), *The Wrong Man*, *Vertigo* and *North by Northwest*.

Paramount's refusal to back *Psycho* forced Alfred Hitchcock to take a risk and finance the film himself. As it turned out it was a risk worth taking. Not only did he make a lot of money from his cut of the box-office receipts, in 1962 he swapped all rights to *Psycho* and to his TV series for around 150,000 shares of MCA (Universal's owner) stock, making him the third-largest shareholder in the company and a multimillionaire.

After *Psycho*, Alfred Hitchcock moved his film-making operation to Universal, where he made *The Birds*, *Marnie*, *Torn Curtain*, *Topaz* (1969), *Frenzy* (1972) and *Family Plot* (1976). At the height of his career Alfred Hitchcock had made a film virtually every year, but as he moved into his late sixties and seventies he gradually slowed down.

To honour his eightieth birthday, the American Film Institute gave Alfred Hitchcock a special award, and in the British New Year's Honours List of 1980 he received a knighthood. Alfred Hitchcock died in his sleep on 29 April 1980.

hitchcock and the auteur theory

Alfred Hitchcock is one of the most critically analysed directors in the history of the cinema. In the British Film Institute library there are literally hundreds of books and articles attempting to unravel and understand the complexities of his films. However, the serious study of film is still a fairly recent phenomenon.

Up until the 1950s, Hollywood cinema was relegated to the status of 'low culture'. This was because the industrial system of Hollywood production, which involved lots of people in making a film for a mass audience in order to gain maximum profit, was considered by most as incompatible with the conventional view of 'art'. The cinema was assigned the status of 'mass entertainment', in contrast to the serious 'high brow' arts of literature, classical music and painting, and was thus not considered to be worthy of serious critical attention.

However, things started to change, in France, in the period after the Second World War. The screening of all Hollywood films had been banned in France during the Nazi occupation. Therefore, in the early post-war years, many of the Hollywood films produced between 1940 and 1945 were screened in quick succession, particularly in the Parisian cinéclubs. Frequenting these clubs was a group of young intellectuals, namely François Truffaut, Eric Rohmer, Claude Chabrol and Jean-Luc Godard, all of whom eventually wrote for the influential film magazine *Cahiers du cinéma* under the leadership of André Bazin.

Cahiers du cinéma revolutionised the critical appraisal of Hollywood cinema. Articles appeared which, for the first time, seriously analysed popular Hollywood **genres** such as the western and the gangster, and writers studied the themes and styles of Hollywood directors such as Alfred Hitchcock, Howard Hawks and John Ford.

The *Cahiers* critics labelled directors such as Alfred Hitchcock as **auteurs** – which translates as author or artist. The origins of *Cahiers*' '*politique des auteurs*' can be found in a seminal article written by Alexandre Astruc in 1948:

> The cinema is quite simply becoming a means of expression, just as all the other arts have been before it, and in particular painting and the novel. After having been successively a fairground attraction, an amusement analogous to boulevard theatre, or a means of preserving the images of an era, it is gradually

'a consistent development, deepening, and clarification'

> becoming a language. By language, I mean a form in which and by which an artist can express his thoughts, however abstract they may be, or translate his obsessions exactly as he does in the contemporary essay or novel.
>
> *printed in Graham ed., 1968, pp. 17–18*

In 1951 Alexandre Astruc produced an article on Alfred Hitchcock's film *Under Capricorn* for the first issue of *Cahiers du cinéma*. And in the second edition of the magazine Jean-Luc Godard, in a review of *Strangers on a Train*, pronounced Alfred Hitchcock one of the greatest directors of the cinema. In 1954 *Cahiers du cinéma* dedicated a whole issue to Alfred Hitchcock, and in 1957 Eric Rohmer and Claude Chabrol published the first book analysing Alfred Hitchcock's films.

By the mid 1960s the influence of the auteur approach to Alfred Hitchcock had reached American and English critics, and Robin Wood was asking, 'Why should we take Hitchcock seriously?' (Wood, 1989, p. 55). The answer he provided was:

> First, then, one might point to the *unity* of Hitchcock's work, and the nature of that unity. I mean of course something much deeper than the fact that he frequently reverts to mystery thrillers for his material; I also mean something broader and much more complex than the fact that certain themes – such as the celebrated 'exchange of guilt' – turn up again and again, although that is a part of it. Not only in theme – in style, method, moral attitude, assumptions about the nature of life – Hitchcock's mature films reveal, on inspection, a consistent development, deepening, and clarification.
>
> *Wood, 1989, p. 64*

The auteur approach to Alfred Hitchcock certainly enables one to place *Psycho* within the context of his other films. Recognisable themes in the film include the influence of the dead over the living, the transference of guilt, the punishment of sexual transgression and the influence of the mother figure. Recurring visual motifs that can be linked to other Hitchcock films include mirrors, birds and eyes, while voyeurism is both a visual motif and a structuring device within the film. (See Narrative & Form and Style for further analysis of the narrative themes and stylistic devices in *Psycho*.)

However, the auteur approach is not without its critics, and the theory has become the subject of its own intense debate. Those who subscribe to it believe that it offers a way of understanding the whole oeuvre of a director's work; that it provides an interesting perspective from which to 'read' a film for those who are aware of a director's previous works; and that it assigns the cinema its rightful status as an 'art form'. Those who disagree argue that the auteur approach ends up creating a pantheon of great directors and neglects the films of others; that it is impossible to locate the 'meaning of a film' with the director as sole creator when it is a collaborative medium that employs so many different people in creative roles; and that it merely creates a 'cult of personality'. This is certainly true when one considers the range of creative input from the people who worked alongside Alfred Hitchcock on *Psycho* – from Joseph Stefano, who contributed many of the ideas for the screenplay when the film was being developed, right through to Bernard Herrmann who advised Alfred Hitchcock to use music to make the shower murder scene more effective.

As film theory has developed over the years, theorists have also condemned the auteur theory as 'too prescriptive', arguing that it asserts the film-maker as 'creator of all meaning' and thus denies the work of the spectator in finding their own meaning in the film.

The controversies surrounding the auteur theory can unfortunately mask its significance. The *politique des auteurs* marked a key moment in film history. It was a founding part of modern film theory, which evolved into the discipline of film studies. The auteur approach is perhaps best now considered as one way in which to approach the study of a film, rather than as a method for deciding whether a particular director is good, bad or indifferent.

Whether one agrees with the auteur approach or not, the fact that Alfred Hitchcock was one of the most important and influential directors in the development of the cinema is irrefutable. Truffaut said:

one of the most heavily analysed texts in film studies

> If Hitchcock, to my way of thinking, outranks the rest, it is because he is the most complete film-maker of all. He is not merely an expert at some specific aspect of cinema, but an all-round specialist, who excels at every image, each shot, and every scene.
>
> *Truffaut, 1985, p. 18*

conclusion

Just as Alfred Hitchcock has had massive amounts of critical and theoretical attention lavished upon his work, so too, *Psycho* must be one of the most heavily analysed texts in film studies literature. The analysis that exists demonstrates that a hugely popular film can be worthy of critical attention – precisely because of what it can tell us about the society and culture that produced it. The objectives of this Note therefore are threefold. It will explore why *Psycho* had such an impact on audiences and the film industry on its release; analyse how a film creates meaning for its spectators through technique and style; and evaluate how *Psycho* relates to the society that produced it.

narrative & form

film narrative

The history of the cinema has been inextricably bound up with narrative. And yet this is not the only path it could have taken as a medium. When the first films of the Lumière brothers were shown, they were recordings of real-life events such as the train arriving at a station or workers leaving the factory. Initially, films were screened at fairgrounds or as part of 'music hall' entertainment, and their novelty factor was that no one had ever seen proper moving images before 1895. However, it was clear the novelty of the technology would not last for very long.

The most prosperous use of moving-image technology soon became associated with telling stories. The novel and the theatre were already well-established mediums of entertainment at the turn of the twentieth century and the very first narrative films did little more than record tableaux of action, as they would have been played out on the stage. But gradually, over the course of twenty years, the cinema developed its own way of telling stories.

THE DEVELOPMENT OF NARRATIVE IN HOLLYWOOD

The way in which the most popular form of cinema has developed is tied closely to the industrial and economic organisation of Hollywood. Between 1895 and 1914 the techniques of film-making were being developed in both America and Europe. However, the First World War halted film production in Europe, and during this period the American film industry started to dominate world cinema. One reason for this was the sheer size of the American population. Films made in America recouped their production costs at the American domestic box office and could then be sold cheaply around the world, making it difficult for European film-makers to compete financially in their own countries.

As the silent era of film-making came to a close at the end of the 1920s it was the Hollywood **studios**, with the backing of Wall Street, that could first afford to make the substantial investments needed to wire the studios and the cinemas for sound. Introducing sound to the cinema affected not just studio and cinema technology, however. The cinematic 'language' of editing, framing, lighting and acting styles also had to adapt to the new era. As the Hollywood studios held such a position of international dominance in the cinema, it followed that the language and conventions of sound film-making that Hollywood evolved to suit its purposes became the most influential around the world.

The Hollywood conventions for storytelling in the sound cinema, which became known as **Classical Hollywood Narrative**, evolved between the late 1920s and the mid 1930s. As **vertically integrated** businesses, the studios' main aim was to make money by entertaining people. Therefore, as a narrative formula successful with audiences became established it was consolidated.

CLASSICAL HOLLYWOOD NARRATIVE

The basic conventions of Classical Hollywood Narrative cinema can be listed as:

■ **equilibrium/disruption/re-equilibrium**

■ **closure**

■ **cause and effect**

■ the **protagonist**

It might seem rather obvious to say that a Classical Hollywood Narrative film has a beginning, a middle and an end. But one has to stop and consider why this is so. The pattern of equilibrium/disruption/re-equilibrium describes the basic structure of a film made in the Classical Hollywood Narrative style. Equilibrium is the state of 'balanced calm' that exists in the world of the characters before the 'events' of the film. A disruption takes place that affects the lives of the characters in some way. The film is then all about how the disruption or problem is solved. Finally, the film ends once a 'balanced equilibrium' is regained.

The term closure refers to the way in which a Classical Hollywood Narrative film draws itself to a close. It is similar to re-equilibrium, but

everything in the narrative is resolved

specifically describes how all the 'loose ends' of a story are tied together. In a Classical Hollywood Narrative film everything in the narrative is resolved. Closure is a narrative technique that signals the end of a film and sends an audience away happy. This was vital to Hollywood as an entertainment business because the studios wanted the audience to return for more. Hence the ubiquitous Hollywood 'happy ending'.

Cause and effect describes the way in which the individual scenes of a film are 'stitched together'. Every scene in a Classical Hollywood Narrative film is linked and motivated, and nothing extraneous is shown or discussed. Everything that is presented to the spectator is there for a narrative reason. This helps guide the spectator in their reading of a film. They don't have to decipher what might be important or relevant in what they see and hear. The sifting has already been done for them. Cause and effect was, and is, a vital element of the success of Hollywood films because it makes the narrative so easy to understand.

The role of the protagonist in Classical Hollywood Narrative films, closely linked to the star system, was another key factor of success. The protagonist is the main character in a narrative film, usually the film's hero and star. Most, if not all, of the events in a Classical Hollywood Narrative film revolve around the protagonist. The narrative disruption affects them, they are linked to the chain of cause and effect and their actions bring about the film's closure. The protagonist also usually occupies a central place in the images of the film. The camera keeps them at the centre of the frame, thus encouraging spectator identification. Classical Hollywood Narrative protagonists are always motivated, so that spectators can understand the cause of their actions, and usually they are 'on the side of the angels', i.e. they play the good guy (and invariably they are male). Yet again, the role of the protagonist acts as a guiding force for the spectator who is 'reading' the film. They can identify the protagonist early on and know what to expect from them.

ANALYSING NARRATIVE

Storytelling is a powerful part of most human societies. From the Bible to the plays of Shakespeare, and even to the way in which we recount the events of our day to friends and family, the form of the 'story' provides us with a way in which to communicate. In a bid to understand the way in which stories function, various theorists have analysed storytelling. One such theorist was the Russian linguist Vladimir Propp. In the 1920s he analysed Russian folk tales and found that, whatever their content, they all followed the same basic pattern. His findings thus concluded that there existed certain conventions that structured the way stories were told. These conventions were not 'written down', as folk tales were most commonly passed on verbally from generation to generation.

However, by identifying what the conventions were, Vladimir Propp demonstrated that stories were not told in a 'haphazard' way but that, like language, they had a basic 'grammar'. Vladimir Propp's work has been very influential in film studies. As a theoretical discipline, the study of film seeks to understand how the flickering projection of light on a screen creates meaning that millions of spectators around the world understand. Analysing the structure of narrative is an essential part of this.

When discussing narrative it is necessary to understand the meaning of the word as it is used in film studies. Narrative does not refer to the story. The content, or story, of a film is called the plot. Narrative refers to the way in which the story is told. Therefore, the narrative is part of the form, or the structure, of a film. One analogy might be to compare a film to the engine of a car. Studying narrative is like studying the components of an engine to understand how it makes a car work.

The 'transparent' nature of the conventions of the Classical Hollywood Narrative system accounts largely for its power and success as a narrative tool. Just like a quiet, perfectly engineered engine in a top-of-the-range car, the Classical Hollywood Narrative conventions 'worked away in the background', not drawing attention to themselves, but carrying out their job efficiently. The fact that the conventions are so unobtrusive makes the need to study them even more imperative because they implicitly carry much of the **ideology** of a film (see Contexts: Race, and Contexts: Sex and Gender) in what appears to be a 'natural' way.

All of the narrative conventions discussed above form part of the

> the plot of *Psycho* is fairly straightforward

'language of the cinema' and thus are part of a film's 'form'. Reading a film is like reading a book. As you read this book your brain is working to decode the shapes of letters on the page, to ascertain the relationship of the letters to each other to create words, and from the words to create sentences. The alphabet, grammar and punctuation enable you to make sense of the shapes on the page. The job is also made easier because your brain has learnt to expect certain combinations of letters, words and grammatical constructs.

These same principles can be applied to the work you do when you are reading a film. Narrative conventions provide a framework for your reading. Expectations of the way a film will begin, progress and end and how it will follow a protagonist make watching a film easy and pleasurable.

narrative in psycho

Understanding the way in which the Classical Hollywood Narrative system works is important if one is to understand why *Psycho* had the impact on spectators and the industry that it did when it was released.

PLOT SYNOPSIS

The plot of *Psycho* is fairly straightforward. Marion Crane and her lover Sam Loomis cannot marry because of Sam's debts. When Marion is asked by her boss to bank $40,000 she decides to steal the money. She heads off to the town where Sam lives, but has to turn off the highway at night because of bad weather. She ends up staying at the Bates Motel where she meets the shy owner Norman Bates. Norman and Marion talk about their problems over supper and Marion decides to head back home to return the money. However, as she takes a shower she is murdered by what appears to be Norman's mother. Norman clears away the mess of the murder but he soon finds himself interrogated by a private detective, Arbogast, sent to track down the stolen $40,000, and by Marion's sister Lila, and Sam, who are concerned about Marion's disappearance. When Arbogast tries to approach Norman's mother he too is murdered. And when Sam and Lila try to find out what happened to Marion and

Arbogast they finally discover the truth about the Bates Motel. Lila finds the skeleton of Mrs Bates in the cellar and Sam just stops Norman from murdering Lila, while dressed in his mother's clothes. The story ends with a psychiatrist's explanation of Norman's mental condition and the revelation that Mother's personality has now completely taken over Norman.

NARRATIVE DIFFERENCES IN PSYCHO

The plot of *Psycho*, although controversial for its day, was not necessarily in itself what caused spectators to be profoundly affected by the film. Rather, it was the way the film-makers told the story, using and challenging the narrative conventions that spectators were familiar with, that marked *Psycho* out as a very different film.

The equilibrium at the beginning of *Psycho* relates to the relationship between Marion and Sam. They have to meet in a hotel room to make love because they cannot afford to marry. But Marion is unhappy with this and thus the narrative disruption is set in motion.

When Marion returns to her office after the opening scene in the hotel room, a classic example of cause and effect takes place. As Marion is ruminating over her own misfortune, a rich client called Tom Cassidy comes in with her boss to buy a house with cash for his daughter's wedding present.

An immediate solution to Marion and Sam's problems is thus presented and a narrative chain of cause and effect is set in motion. Marion steals the money and runs away to buy her chance of happiness with Sam. In a conventional narrative one would expect the narrative to stay with Marion and for the film's final re-equilibrium and closure to relate to the stolen money and her marriage to Sam. However, it is *Psycho*'s deviation from this narrative pattern that made it such a challenging film for its time.

While Alfred Hitchcock cannot be credited with the idea of murdering the character of Marion midway through the film (that idea is taken from Robert Bloch's original novel) there are two things that make the death of Marion in the film far more shocking. First of all was the use

'the first part of the story was a red herring'

of the **star** Janet Leigh for the part of Marion Crane. As the director explained:

> In the average production, Janet Leigh would have been given the other role. She would have played the sister who's investigating. It's rather unusual to kill the star in the first third of the film. I purposely killed the star so as to make the killing even more unexpected. As a matter of fact, that's why I insisted that the audiences be kept out of the theaters once the picture had started, because the late-comers would have been waiting to see Janet Leigh after she has disappeared from the screen action.
>
> *Truffaut, 1985, p. 269*

Secondly, the way that the position of the protagonist is set up and then shifts deviates radically from the Classical Hollywood Narrative norm. In the novel Robert Bloch begins with the character of Norman, and thus the narrative is essentially telling Norman's story from the start. Screenwriter Joseph Stefano, however, made the suggestion to start the film with Marion's story and Norman is not introduced until one third of the way through the film. For the first half an hour the spectator's view of narrative events is restricted to Marion's point of view. She is the one the camera first rests on when it trespasses into the motel room she is sharing with Sam, and she is the one that Cassidy flirts with in the office. Once she steals the money the point of view is made even more subjective as the spectator shares her paranoid looks back at the policeman following her, hears the voices in her head as she imagines what people will say when they discover what she's done, and peers through the darkness and the rain with her as the windscreen wipers flick backwards and forwards as she drives towards the Bates Motel.

Once again, Alfred Hitchcock's rationale for doing this was to thwart audience expectations:

> In fact, the first part of the story was a red herring. That was deliberate, you see, to detract the viewer's attention in order to heighten the murder. We purposely made that beginning on the long side, with the bit about the theft and her escape, in order to

the spectator's interest is transferred entirely to Norman

> get the audience absorbed with the question of whether she would or would not be caught. Even that business about the forty thousand dollars was milked to the very end so that the public might wonder what's going to happen to the money.
>
> *Truffaut, 1985, p. 269*

Alfred Hitchcock was renowned for his use of what he called a MacGuffin – the thing that appears to be central to the plot of a film but which, in actual fact, is entirely irrelevant. In *Psycho* the MacGuffin is the money. However, it is not just the fact that Alfred Hitchcock uses a MacGuffin that makes the narrative of *Psycho* unusual. The way that the narrative structure shifts after Marion's murder makes the film particularly complex. After Marion has been stabbed she sinks gradually down into the bath, grabs hold of the shower curtain and falls forward. The protagonist, whose point of view has been exclusively followed by the spectator up until now, is dead and the camera has to detach itself. It follows the flow of Marion's blood as it drains away and then **dissolves** from a **close-up** of the plughole to a close-up of Marion's eye. The camera spirals out from the close-up of the dead staring eye and a **tracking shot** moves out of the bathroom and over to the money. The camera then reframes again to look out of the window up to the Bates house. Offscreen, Norman can be heard shouting to his mother, and then he is seen running down the steps from the house to the motel room.

For the rest of this scene the camera follows the actions of Norman, and the spectator watches as he washes away all traces of the murder. By the time a beam from a passing car moves across Norman's face, startling him, the spectator is already starting to feel concern for Norman's plight (at this stage assuming him to be the dutiful son, protecting his mother). However, the master stroke to ensure that the spectator's interest is transferred entirely to Norman comes when Marion's car suddenly stops as it is sinking into the swamp. Norman looks around nervously, and the spectators, by now rooting for Norman, breathe a collective sigh of relief as the car moves again and disappears entirely into the inky blackness of the swamp.

spectator sympathies are transferred

Norman and the audience
wait for the car to sink as
spectator sympathies are
transferred

From hereon in, the structure of the narrative is fractured and Norman, Lila, Sam and Arbogast each take on the mantle of protagonist at various times. After Marion's car sinks into the swamp the screen **fades** to black. When it fades up again the setting is Sam's hardware store and Lila has arrived to search for Marion. Arbogast also enters the store and says that he too is looking for Marion and the money.

Alfred Hitchcock continues to use the technique of cause and effect to motivate each scene. Arbogast calls Lila to tell her that Marion was at the Bates Motel, that he is going back to question the mother and will be back in an hour. When he doesn't call it motivates Sam and Lila to go to the Bates Motel. As a structuring device, cause and effect makes the progress of the narrative easy to follow.

However, the absence of a clear structure of equilibrium/disruption/re-equilibrium makes narrative closure problematic. The narrative has changed from Marion's quest for marriage to the search for Marion. And as the film progresses it changes yet again to the search for Mrs Bates.

The scene in the courthouse, where a psychiatrist explains Norman's mental condition, has been criticised for seeming rather 'tacked on' and dissatisfying. However, it is not just the rather patronising tone of the psychiatrist's speech that jars. Although he does go some way to explain Norman's actions, there is hardly any mention of Marion's fate at all.

On the surface, the end of the film has very little to do with the beginning and so, in classical narrative terms, closure is not complete.

However, *Psycho* does not close on the psychiatrist's speech. After the psychiatrist finishes his explanation of Norman's condition a policeman comes into the room and says that Norman feels a little chill. The camera **cuts** to a shot of the corridor and the policeman is shown going into a cell with a blanket, while Mother's voice is heard off screen. Another cut follows to reveal Norman sitting in an empty cell, draped in a blanket, and the spectator is made privy to Mother's thoughts via a **voice-over**. The shot of Norman then dissolves into a shot of Marion's car being dredged up from the swamp, and for a brief moment an image of Mother's skull is **superimposed** over the dissolve. This complex ending means that, in effect, there are three separate closures. The first is the

'the end, apparently, in no way replies to the beginning'

'official' ending – fully backed by the presence of society and the law (the courthouse, the sheriff, the psychiatrist) – which tries to contain the antisocial events of the narrative. The shot of Norman/Mother (made particularly unnerving by Norman's slightly smirking facial expression) reinvokes the threat of madness bubbling away underneath the surface of the film, and contradicts the calm tone of the psychiatrist who would like us to believe that the problem has been resolved. Finally, the shot of Marion's car reminds us of the punishment for transgression of society's laws (Marion was a thief and a sexually active unmarried woman). The three endings jostle uneasily with each other and the final mixed image of Norman, Mother and Marion's car exists beyond the boundary set by the reassuring scene in the courthouse. This would have been very unsettling for the spectator, who was used to being sent home from the Hollywood films of the 1950s happy and secure, with a satisfying sense of full narrative closure.

ALTERNATIVE NARRATIVE STRUCTURE

One theorist who has considered the complexity of *Psycho*'s narrative and provides an alternative reading is Raymond Bellour:

> The principle of classical film is well known: the end must reply to the beginning; between one and the other something must be set in order; the last scene frequently recalls the first and constitutes its resolution. *Psycho*'s opaqueness is contradictory in this respect: the end, apparently, in no way replies to the beginning: the psychiatrist's commentary on the case of Norman Bates has little to do with the love scene between Marion and Sam in the Phoenix hotel. The specific obscurity of *Psycho* is thus, above all, a rhetorical obscurity. It denotes the fact that the film, in a sense, contravenes the classical model of narrative.
>
> *Bellour, 1979, p. 105*

Raymond Bellour goes on to say:

> *Psycho* contains two narratives, slipping one under the other, one into the other. (...) The singular genius of the film consists of

narrative in psycho

Norman and Marion's meeting
leads to a shift in the narrative's
structure

Marion's neurosis leads to the psychotic actions of Norman

> indissolubly mixing together the two narratives that it is composed of by using the meeting of the two characters as the means of their substitution.
>
> *Bellour, 1979, pp. 107–109*

Raymond Bellour goes on to how the closure of the film does in fact reply to the film's opening, not in the usual way, where a straightforward re-equilibrium of the plot is established, but in a more complex way whereby the thematic trajectories set in motion by the narrative are closed off.

> The first scene(s) is (are) programmed as a matrix whose elements are distributed throughout the whole text by effects of dispersal, rebound and repetition. (...) In *Psycho*, this process is at first carried out at a very general level. The first scene, through the shift in the **screenplay**, primarily serves as a preparation for the succession of scenes between Marion and Norman: their tête-à-tête in the reception room, the series of shots setting up Norman as apparatus, the murder in the shower. From this is derived, at the end, the scene with the psychiatrist, which resolves not only the enigma, but the (psychic) mystery of the murder: this final scene only replies to the first one at the price of the initial displacement caused by the shift in the screenplay.
>
> *Bellour, 1979, p. 122*

For Raymond Bellour, closure is achieved in *Psycho* because Marion's neurosis, displayed in her active sexual behaviour and her theft of the money, leads to the psychotic actions of Norman – which are adequately explained in the psychiatrist's speech.

Raymond Bellour also analyses how the act of **voyeuristic** looking, instigated at the start of the film by the camera's trespassing gaze into the private room and private life of Marion and Sam, is also answered by the final shots of the film, which show Norman, as Mother, staring directly at the camera and acknowledging that he/she is being watched.

narrative in psycho

NARRATIVE STRUCTURE AND HITCHCOCK AS AUTEUR

Raymond Bellour's analysis demonstrates that narrative structure does not simply have to relate to the events of the plot, but that a film's thematic concerns can also play a part in structuring the form of a film. The way that narrative form and thematic content are bound together in *Psycho* demonstrates Alfred Hitchcock's ingenuity as a film-maker and can be used to support the arguments of those critics who claim him as a cinematic **auteur** (see Background: Hitchcock and the Auteur Theory).

If one carries out an auteur study of Alfred Hitchcock's work, then voyeurism is one of the principal themes to emerge in his films of the late 1950s and early 1960s. Both *Rear Window* and *Vertigo* are constructed around characters who look. L.B. Jeffries in *Rear Window* is a photographer confined to his room with a broken leg, who passes the time spying on his neighbours across the street. And in *Vertigo*, Scottie is a private detective hired by a friend to watch and follow his wife.

Voyeurism is endemic throughout *Psycho*. The film opens with a camera meandering over the skyline of Phoenix. The camera gradually descends and tracks in to the window of a motel room where it spies on Marion and Sam. Once Marion has stolen the money and is on the run to Fairvale to meet Sam she is watched for a long time by a policeman. Then when she gets to the Bates Motel she is spied on by Norman through a peephole in the wall of his parlour. The close-up of Norman's bulging eye is soon replaced by the close-up of Marion's dead eye. Norman is then the one under surveillance from Arbogast, Lila and Sam, and when Mother is finally discovered, the horror of her appearance is accentuated by the light bulb casting swinging shadows over her empty eye sockets. The closing shot of *Psycho*, of Norman/Mother staring out directly at the audience, acknowledging that he/she is being watched by the policemen and psychiatrist and by the audience thus makes sense within the thematic schemata of the film and within a wider understanding of Alfred Hitchcock's oeuvre as director/auteur.

The way that *Psycho*'s narrative is structured around watching and being watched also serves to draw attention to the process of the film's **enunciation**. Most Classical Hollywood Narrative films used stylistic techniques to hide the 'nuts and bolts' of a film's construction. This meant that Classical Hollywood Narrative films usually appeared to unravel seamlessly on the screen, without appearing to be told by anyone. Hitchcock, however, wants the spectator to be aware of their role as 'watchers' of the film, and in so doing he also draws attention to his role as the manipulative author and **enunciator** of the text, signifying his own authorial presence.

conclusion

The reading of *Psycho*'s narrative demonstrates how Alfred Hitchcock challenged many of the conventions of the Classical Hollywood Narrative system. The fact that he did this and still created a film that was phenomenally popular with audiences throughout the world is nothing short of remarkable because most formal and stylistic challenges within the various mediums of art take place only on the margins of the mainstream.

Alfred Hitchcock was a true innovator though, and it is probably the case that the unsettling effects of *Psycho*, which sent audiences shell-shocked out on to the streets after the film, had as much to do with the film's splintering of narrative, uneasy closure and reflections on the act of watching as with the macabre storyline and gruesome murders.

Although Alfred Hitchcock was often self-deprecating in interviews and liked to create a public persona for himself as nothing more than the mischievous 'master of suspense', he was one of the few directors who, after working in cinema for forty years, fully understood the power of the techniques of his medium.

Psycho is not really a film about Marion and Norman and murder at all – in fact the whole plot could be taken as one huge MacGuffin. What the narrative of *Psycho* is really about is the mechanics and politics of watching – which is at the heart of the cinematic experience. With the horrific murder scene in the shower at the very centre of the film, perhaps Alfred Hitchcock was really challenging spectators to see just how far they would go with their own voyeuristic behaviour. The fact

conclusion

that *Psycho* is often credited with spawning the 'slasher' sub-**genre** of horror films (see Background: Reading *Psycho*) and that from the 1960s onwards screen violence increased to the point where it became the focus of wider discussions about violence in society is perhaps indicative of just what Alfred Hitchcock had tapped into with *Psycho*.

Made in 1959, *Psycho* was on the cusp of the transition between Classical Hollywood Narrative cinema and modern cinema.

> Quite an abundant literature has stressed the fact that *Psycho* not only stands for an important turn in the career of its director, but also that the film in content and style does not completely bare the structure of a traditional Hollywood film. In this sense *Psycho* stands somewhere between the classical and the modern cinema; in fact it could be regarded as one of the important transitional films of the last years of the Fifties.
>
> Hesling, 1987

Many of the new generation of film-makers who began to emerge in Hollywood in the 1960s and 1970s, including Francis Ford Coppola, Martin Scorsese and Oliver Stone, started to experiment in their own way with the manner in which film narratives could be told. However, Alfred Hitchcock had laid some of the groundwork already with *Psycho*. From the days of *Blackmail*, when he was one of the first to innovate with film sound, right through to the narrative challenges of *Psycho*, Alfred Hitchcock proved himself to be one of the most important and influential directors in the history of the cinema.

style

Film style is usually understood to refer to the visual and aural elements of a film. However, style can also refer to a film's narrative structure. The narrative style of *Psycho* has already been discussed in Narrative & Form.

classical hollywood narrative style

A film's style is constructed from **mise-en-scène cinematography**, sound and editing. In the **Classical Hollywood Narrative** cinema the job of film style was to serve the narrative. Mise-en-scène and cinematography were meant to be functional. Set designs indicated the correct time and place for the action, costume designs represented the type of character an actor was playing, lighting was there simply to light the action clearly and the camera was moved only to reframe and follow the action. No attention was drawn to the camera's role as mediator.

Likewise, although the job of the soundtrack in cueing audience expectations and emotion was very important, spectators were not meant to be consciously aware of it. Finally, in order to compensate for the fragmentation of time and space caused by editing, a system of **continuity editing** evolved. Spatial continuity was achieved with a variety of techniques, including the **180° rule**, the **35° rule**, **establishing shot**, and the pattern of **shot/reverse shot** for dialogue scenes. **Eyeline-match** and **match–on–action** were two methods that ensured edits were motivated and thus virtually invisible to the spectator, while **overlapping sound** worked to smooth over the potentially disruptive transitions between scenes.

Editing also constructs the time frame of a film. Nearly all films condense

hitchcock's style

real time into 'reel time', so that narrative events that might take place over a day, a year or a lifetime can be shown in ninety minutes. Types of edit became associated with particular time frames in the Classical Hollywood Narrative cinema to ensure that spectators would understand the temporal logic of a film. **Cuts** were used within scenes to represent continuous time, while **fades** and **dissolves** were used to signal the end of a scene and indicate the passing of time.

Hollywood developed the Classical Hollywood Narrative style in the commercial era of the **studio system**, firm in the belief that audiences wanted good stories and **stars**, and were not interested in the intricacies of set design, camera movement, editing or soundtrack composition.

alfred hitchcock's style

Working within Hollywood meant that Alfred Hitchcock made use of many of the stylistic conventions of the Classical Hollywood Narrative cinema. However, from the beginning of his career Alfred Hitchcock also loved to experiment with cinematic techniques and he was renowned for his stylish set pieces. In *Notorious* he elaborately tracked in from a **long shot** of a party taken at the top of some stairs, right down into an extreme **close-up** of a key in Ingrid Bergman's hand; and in *Strangers on a Train* he had the villain, Bruno, sit completely still in the middle of a crowd watching a tennis match, while everyone else's head was turning from side to side. Other Hitchcock films were set up specifically as stylistic challenges. *Rope* was set in one room and was filmed without edits in nearly one continuous **tracking shot** (apart from some hidden editing transitions between the different reels of the film); and the action of *Lifeboat* (1944) was set entirely on a small boat.

Alfred Hitchcock had to make *Psycho* with his own money because Paramount, the studio he was contracted to at the time, refused to finance it (see Background: The Production of *Psycho*). Therefore, he had more freedom than usual to add stylistic flourishes to his film. Alfred Hitchcock's style of working was fairly unusual. He spent a lot of time in pre-production and liked meticulously to plan every aspect of his films. During the pre-production of *Psycho* Alfred Hitchcock spent five

loved to plan his films out in his mind

weeks in story conferences with writer Joseph Stefano. During those meetings,

> Stefano perceived that the way to grasp Hitchcock's imagination was to conceptualise and verbalise the story in terms of visuals. According to Stefano, 'He was not interested in characters or motivation at all. That was the writer's job. If I said, "I'd like to give the girl an air of desperation," he'd say, "Fine, fine." But when I said, "In the opening of the film, I'd like a helicopter shot over the city, then go right up to the seedy hotel where Marion is spending her lunch hour with Sam," he said, "We'll go right into the window!" That sort of thing excited him.'
>
> *Rebello, 1998, p. 41*

Once the script had been written, Alfred Hitchcock and Joseph Stefano set about breaking it down into the screenplay, which acted as a blueprint for production and included instructions for all of the camera shots. From this, storyboards could be made up.

Alfred Hitchcock loved to plan his films out in his mind, and felt that this was the most creative part of the film-making process.

> Once Hitchcock and Stefano had completed the breakdown, it was all over but the shooting. 'We had lunch and toasted the project with champagne,' said Stefano. 'He looked very sad, and said, "The picture's over. Now I have to go and put it on film." '
>
> *Rebello, 1998, p. 50*

psycho's mise-en-scène

Alfred Hitchcock's meticulous planning meant that nothing in the film's mise-en-scène was there by accident. The Bates house was created by production designers Robert Clatworthy and Joseph Hurley. It was an original design, although probably influenced by Edward Hopper's 1925 painting *The House by the Railroad*. Alfred Hitchcock claims that the house was based on the type of Gothic architecture that existed in California at the time.

psycho's mise-en-scène

> I did not set out to reconstruct an old-fashioned Universal horror-picture atmosphere. I simply wanted to be accurate, and there is no question but that both the house and the motel are authentic reproductions of the real thing.
>
> *Truffaut, 1985, p. 269*

The Bates house becomes one of the most significant aspects of the film's mise-en-scène. When seen through the window after Marion has been murdered the house is dark and forbidding and clouds scurry along behind it ominously. Saul Bass said:

> I matted in a time-lapse footage of a moonlit, cloudy sky. The clouds moved at a faster than normal rate. For the few seconds at a time that you saw the scene, you were not aware that the sky was moving at that rate because you tended to concentrate on the house. But you came away with the feeling it was strange. You didn't know why; it just was.
>
> *Bass, 1977, p. 326–7*

The house has already become synonymous with the tyrannical presence of Mother, mainly because Marion hears Mother's voice booming from there when Mother forbids Norman to invite Marion to supper at the house.

Seen through the motel room window after the shower murder, the house is dark except for two bright lights that resemble eyes, perhaps signifying Mother's watchful presence. The fact that the old Bates house is perched on a slight hill and thus looks down on the modern motel that Norman runs means that it also becomes a visual metaphor for the dominance of the past over the present and the dead over the living, a theme that exists in many Hitchcock films (see Background: Hitchcock and the Auteur Theory).

The design of each set in the film contributes to the way in which scenes can be read by the spectator. The bathroom where the murder is carried out is stark and clinical.

The Bates house symbolises
the power of the past over the
present and the dead over the
living – a key theme in Alfred
Hitchcock's work

psycho's mise-en-scène

> Hitchcock disdained the cliché of staging suspense sequences against the usual set pieces of the dark, haunted house. Thus Stefano writes [in the screenplay]: 'The white brightness ... is almost blinding.' Production designer Clatworthy also recalls Hitchcock's enjoining set decorator George Milo to make certain that the bathroom fixtures gleamed.
>
> *Rebello, 1998, p. 70*

The brutal stabbing, carried out in the innocuous, everyday setting of the bathroom went against the Hollywood conventions of horror, where characters were usually attacked in dark, forbidding places and this made the murder even more shocking for the spectator. The everyday details of the bathroom are contrasted further with Norman's parlour behind the office, where the conversation between Norman and Marion takes place. What seems to be an innocent chat over a supper of sandwiches and milk takes on an ominous tone because of the details of the set design.

The room is lit only by lamps that cast shadows across the room. Stuffed birds and lots of heavy furniture crowd the parlour, making it appear claustrophobic and threatening. The birds are particularly significant, and not only because of Norman's proclaimed interest in taxidermy. When Norman leans forward and talks to Marion about his mother the shot is taken from a **low angle** and a large bird of prey is suspended in an attacking position above Norman's head. As Norman gets more agitated about Marion's suggestion that Mother be sent to an institution the angle changes to a closer shot, and this time a bird with its sharp beak in profile is included in the frame, to the left of Norman's face. Then as Marion stands to bid Norman goodnight a crow is included in the shot, again in profile, with its knife-shaped beak seemingly about to attack her. The birds can be read as symbolic of Mother, both in their 'stuffed state' and also in the way their beady eyes stare unblinkingly at Marion and Norman, again representing Mother's watchful presence. Alfred Hitchcock also provides us with a connotation for the stuffed owl seen in the background.

psycho's mise-en-scène style

birds recur as a symbol throughout the film

> Owls belong to the night world; they are watchers, and this appeals to Perkins' masochism. He knows the birds and he knows that they're watching him all the time. He can see his own guilt reflected in their knowing eyes.
>
> *Truffaut, 1985, p. 282*

Birds recur as a symbol throughout the film. Marion's surname is Crane and she comes from the town of Phoenix. The bedroom of cabin number one has pictures of birds on the wall, one of which Norman knocks off when he is cleaning up after the murder. And when Lila stands outside Sam's hardware store, as he drives off to the Bates Motel to look for Norman, the shadow of garden rakes forms the menacing shape of bird-like talons behind her.

Alfred Hitchcock uses many other symbolic objects within *Psycho*'s mise-en-scène that can be related back to the film's themes. An explanation of the painting Norman has placed over the hole in the wall he uses to spy on Marion is given by Barbara Creed.

> The painting (...) is that of *Susanna and the Elders*, a fictional story set during the Jewish Exile in Babylon; it is particularly interesting in relation to voyeurism. Two elders conceive a passion for Susanna whom they spy on when she bathes in the garden. (...) The painting depicts the moment where they apprehend her, trying to hold her semi-naked struggling body. *Susanna and the Elders* points to man's voyeurism and desire to punish woman for her supposed sexual sins. Before removing it from the wall, Norman stares for a moment at this painting, as if the scene it portrayed matched his own private phantasy.
>
> *Creed, 1993, p. 146*

Aside from **voyeurism**, another key theme in *Psycho* relates to the split between good and evil. This theme is inscribed in the film from the opening title sequence, which shows graphical bars moving horizontally and vertically across the screen, coming together and then splitting apart again. Obviously Norman's personality is split to the extreme between

psycho's mise-en-scène

Norman's stuffed birds keep
their beady eyes on the events
at the Bates Motel

good and evil and between son and mother, but even Marion is shown to have a propensity for both good and evil with her theft of the money and then decision to return it.

Mirrors are used throughout the mise-en-scène of *Psycho* to symbolise the duplicitous divisions of personality. When Marion uses the ladies' room at the garage where she exchanges her car, she counts out the cash she needs for the new car in front of a mirror. And the mirror is a central feature of the Bates Motel office, in which Marion, Arbogast, Sam and Lila are all reflected when they first meet Norman. Finally, when Lila snoops around the Bates house and goes into Mother's room, her reflection is caught in a double mirror effect, causing her, and the spectator, to jump with fright.

The mirror images seen throughout the film are extended to the doubling of characters, another theme used extensively in Alfred Hitchcock's work (see Background: Hitchcock and the Auteur Theory). Lila looks very similar to Marion, although that is understandable because she is meant to be her sister, but Sam and Norman are also very similar in appearance, something which is drawn attention to in the scene where Sam stands opposite Norman across the check-in desk and questions him about the motel. Raymond Bellour, in his article 'Psychosis, Neurosis, Perversion' even points out that Marion and Norman are virtually interchangeable names, save for the letter 'i'.

Alfred Hitchcock also uses many established cultural conventions to create meaning for the spectators of the film. When Marion is first seen in the hotel room with Sam at the beginning of the film she is wearing a white bra and slip. When she returns to the office she is also wearing a white dress and carrying a white handbag. However, when the spectator next sees her, in her room after she has stolen the money and is packing to run away, she is wearing a black bra and slip, puts on a dark outfit and picks up a black bag. Costume is thus used as a way of symbolising her descent into evil, using the cultural shorthand of black and white to represent good and evil.

Lighting is also used expressively. The first part of the film, when Marion is in Phoenix, is lit evenly and the scenes take place in daylight. Once

psycho's mise-en-scène

Marion gets to the Bates Motel though, the lighting is much more subdued. Norman's office, parlour and house are all lit with table lamps, which cast faint shadows. Although, as mentioned earlier, a stylistic counterpoint is created between the gloom of the house and the brightness of the bathroom where the murder takes place, thwarting conventional expectations, most of the second half of the film takes place in a grey half-light. (The only exceptions to this are when Lila and Sam visit the sheriff's brightly lit house and go to church on a sunny morning with the sheriff and his wife.)

However, the most stylised use of lighting is saved to heighten the drama and horror of the moment when Mrs Bates is finally revealed. As Lila turns Mrs Bates round in her chair, the horror of her discovery leads her to thrash out and hit the naked light bulb above her. The swinging light bulb casts an eerie light over Lila's distressed face, Norman dressed in Mother's clothes and Mrs Bates's skull. Normally, once the 'monstrous' object in horror films is finally revealed it is never visually as frightening as the thing imagined, but the lighting effect used here seems to animate the skull, giving it an even more horrific effect.

The other people who contribute greatly to the mise-en-scène of a film are the actors. Alfred Hitchcock gained notoriety in his career for dismissing actors as 'cattle' and it was acknowledged that he was far more interested in the techniques of film-making than in performance. However, the memories of the actors that worked with him on *Psycho* illustrate both Alfred Hitchcock's working method and the way that they worked to create their character. Janet Leigh remembers,

> We had several meetings before we started *Psycho* – he told me what he needed from me for *his* picture. He said, 'I'm not going to tell you how to act. If I didn't think you could act, I wouldn't have you in my picture. I'm telling you the qualities I need, where I need certain points (...) as long as your concept of her doesn't interfere with what I need from her, do whatever you want.'

'magazine cover boy to play a transvestite'

> I read the book. I saw that she was really a shabby, mousy little woman. She wasn't in any way glamorous or anything. So we chose clothes that she could have afforded. We didn't have a dressmaker do them; we just went out and bought clothes that she could have bought on her salary. And I didn't have the hairdresser do my hair, I did it myself as she would: she couldn't afford a beauty parlour.
>
> *Leigh, 1970, p. 69*

Before Anthony Perkins was cast as Norman Bates he was a teen pin-up. As Stephen Rebello says:

> The willingness of a late-fifties fan magazine cover boy to play a transvestite – even under the direction of Hitchcock – was admirable. The fifties were conservative years and perhaps few other actors might have taken the risk.
>
> *Rebello, 1998, p. 59*

The casting of Anthony Perkins as Norman gave the character a softness and vulnerability that was added to by the actor's suggestion that Norman chew nervously on candy throughout the film. When he first runs down from the house to meet Marion, Norman appears to be just an awkward, gangling young man, with his hands thrust deep into his pockets and his shoulders hunched against the rain. However, once he becomes riled about Marion's suggestion that Mother should perhaps be sent away somewhere, an intensity comes into the performance. He sits forward on his chair and his expression and tone of voice become more dangerous as he tells Marion that we all go a little mad sometimes.

Anthony Perkin's portrayal of Norman Bates contributes to the way the spectator reads the mise-en-scène of *Psycho*'s images, along with the set design, costume design and lighting effects. Throughout every scene of the film all of this visual information combines to create the text that the spectator reads. Alfred Hitchcock, working alongside all the other creative personnel in the production team, orchestrates everything to create the overall impact that is required.

black and white would not show the gore

psycho's cinematography

The style of the image track of a film is not constructed from mise-en-scène alone. The camera's cinematography also adds meaning to every shot, which the spectator then transcribes in their reading.

Psycho was filmed in black and white at a time when most Hollywood films were being made in colour. There were two reasons behind this decision, one of which was budgetary constraints. In 1959 it was still much cheaper to film with black and white stock, and Alfred Hitchcock had a budget of only $800,000 for *Psycho* because of Paramount's refusal.to back the film (see Background: The Production of *Psycho*). The second reason was to appease the censors. Alfred Hitchcock knew that he had a much better chance of getting the film passed in black and white because it would not show the gore of the blood in the murder scenes.

Whatever the practical reasons for choosing black and white stock, the result had an undeniable stylistic effect on the film. In the 1940s and 1950s, when colour was first introduced into film-making, the bright Technicolor stock was reserved for musicals and escapist fantasy films such as *The Wizard of Oz* (1939). However, black and white stock was still used for **genres** set in contemporary reality, such as the gangster and the thriller. By the late 1950s, in order to compete with the new medium of television, which at that time was broadcast in black and white, most Hollywood feature films were being made in colour. This meant that *Psycho*'s black and white stock would have marked it out as different. Coupled with the downmarket setting of seedy motels and the plot concerning everyday working characters such as Sam the store owner and Marion the secretary, the black and white cinematography gives *Psycho* an air of ordinariness and 'realism' that makes the events at the Bates Motel even more horrific. Alfred Hitchcock knew he had audiences thinking this could happen to anyone, in any town in America, and that is one of the reasons the film so frightened spectators who were more used to fantasy horror films about zombies and vampires.

Through his wide experience of film-making, gained over forty years, Alfred Hitchcock also knew how to manipulate the camera in order to manipulate the audience. On set Alfred Hitchcock never even needed to look through the camera. 'Well, why should I? I know what lens is on. I know where the camera is. So I know what I'm getting!' Hitchcock said to rookie director Curtis Harrington, who was once given the opportunity to shadow Alfred Hitchcock on set (Leigh and Nickens, 1995, p. 50).

For *Psycho*, Alfred Hitchcock chose to use an unusual 50-millimetre lens.

> On the 35-millimetre cameras of the day, such lenses gave the closest approximation to human vision technically possible. 'He wanted the camera being the eyes of the audience all the time, to let them [view the action] as if they were seeing it with their own eyes,' script supervisor Marshal Schlom explained. Again, Hitchcock reinforced the sensation of voyeurism – of 'cruel eyes studying you', as Norman Bates puts it – that permeates the entire film.
>
> *Rebello, 1998, p. 93*

Alfred Hitchcock's desire to heighten spectators' awareness that they were voyeuristic watchers was reinforced through the framing of shots and movement of the camera. Classical Hollywood Narrative films did not usually draw attention to the position or movement of the camera (see Style: Classical Hollywood Narrative Style); the norm was to film straight on from a human perspective and to move the camera only to reframe as the actors moved.

Alfred Hitchcock, however, was not afraid to innovate with low angle close-ups, extreme **high angle** shots and a tracking camera when he wanted to create a specific position for the spectator. When Arbogast begins to break down Norman's defence that Marion never visited the motel, by comparing a sample of Marion's handwriting with the signature she gives of Marie Samuels in Norman's visitors' book, there is

spectators right in the centre of the action

a cut to a low angle close-up of Norman's face looking at the signature. The screen is filled with Norman's chin chewing on his candy with increased intensity so that the spectator is presented with a striking visual manifestation of Norman's guilt and fear.

Earlier in the film, when Alfred Hitchcock wanted the spectator to identify with Marion's position, he took the camera right into the shower, cutting between shots of Marion showering and a low angle subjective shot of the shower head, despite the technical difficulties this created.

> Hitchcock challenged cameraman Russell and his production team by devising a point-of-view shot to heighten audience identification with Janet Leigh. He wanted to show water pulsing out the shower head straight toward the camera (...) 'Everyone's first and obvious question was, "If we shoot right at it, how are we going to keep the lens dry?" [noted script supervisor Schlom]. Mr. Hitchcock said, "Put the camera *there* with a long lens and block off the inner holes on the shower head so they won't spout water." By using the longer lens, we could get back a little farther, shoot a little tighter and the water appeared to have hit the lens but actually sprayed past it. The guys on the sides got a little soaked but, meanwhile, we got the shot.'
>
> *Rebello, 1998, p. 114*

By cutting in with close-ups, Alfred Hitchcock could place spectators right in the centre of the action. However, there were also times when he wanted to pull the spectators out and give them a dispassionate, omnipotent, high-angle view.

As Marion's killer flees from the bathroom, there is a cut to a brief high-angle shot above the shower, removing the spectator from the frenzy of the stabbing. Alfred Hitchcock repeats this use of a high angle in the next murder scene when Arbogast is killed. As Arbogast enters the Bates house, Alfred Hitchcock cuts between medium close-ups of Arbogast's face and shots of the interior of the house as he looks around. He then begins to walk up the stairs and the camera tracks slowly back in front of him. There is a close-up of the bedroom door

unusual camera movements

opening slightly and then a cut back to Arbogast, gradually building the suspense of the sequence. Alfred Hitchcock then cuts to an extreme high-angle shot of the landing, showing 'Mrs Bates' rushing out and attacking Arbogast.

While the high angle obviously functions to hide the identity of the killer (and the same angle is used later when Norman carries Mother downstairs to the cellar), it also provides an alternate position for the spectator, shifting them between positions of involvement and observation. This in turn creates a powerful effect of fear. Not only is the spectator made to identify with the person under attack, they also experience the horror of watching the attack – this creates a double-whammy effect and is perhaps yet another reason why *Psycho* had such an impact on spectators on its release.

Camera movements are used in a variety of ways in *Psycho*. When Lila goes in search of Mrs Bates, Alfred Hitchcock cuts between **medium shots** of Lila and a forward tracking camera, which judders slightly from left to right in an almost hand-held style, representing Lila's subjective **point of view** as she walks towards the house. The effect is to position the spectator with Lila, who is putting herself in grave danger, just as Marion and Arbogast did before her.

Other unusual camera movements are used to draw attention to something significant, for example, when Lila is snooping around in Mrs Bates's room a quickly jolting **zoom** is used to focus in on the folded hands on the dressing table. This communicates something of Lila's anxiety and also marks the hands out as significant as they act as a precursor of the mummified remains Lila is about to discover in the cellar.

However, Alfred Hitchcock reserved what appears to be his most elaborate camera movement to enhance the impact of Arbogast's death on screen. As Arbogast is struck by Mother's knife he falls backwards down the stairs and the camera follows him. Marshal Schlom explains:

> we did [it] by shooting a moving background plate using the monopod without Marty [Martin Balsam who played Arbogast].

psycho's cinematography

'It allows the viewer to become a peeping Tom'

> Later, we had Marty, sitting in a gimbal, flailing in front of a standard rear-projection screen.
>
> *Rebello, 1998, p. 125*

Alfred Hitchcock's camera movements in *Psycho* did more than just exploit technique to create exciting set pieces. There are times in the film when the director appears to allow the camera to wander completely detached from characters and character point of view. *Psycho* opens with an extreme long shot of a city which a title tells us is Phoenix, Arizona. The camera **pans** right across the city skyline, gradually moving in towards the buildings until it picks out one window. The camera tracks in through the open window, pans across the room and finally comes to rest on Marion, laying on the bed. 'It allows the viewer to become a Peeping Tom,' said Alfred Hitchcock (Truffaut, 1985, p. 266). The camera's movement also draws attention to the fact that the spectator is being guided into this particular story. Another example of the wandering camera occurs in the scene when Marion is changing in her room after she has stolen the money – the camera moves away from watching her get dressed and instead pans across to the envelope of money on the bed and then across to her packed suitcase; and the camera wanders yet again in the scene after Marion has been murdered, when the camera detaches itself from the observation of Marion's dead body, tracks out of the bathroom, over to the money on the bedside table and then moves again over to the window where the spectator hears Norman's distressed shouts to Mother.

At moments like these, Alfred Hitchcock is drawing attention away from the action of the actors and towards his own role as **enunciator** of the film. As Kenneth Johnson remarks,

> When the camera so wanders, we become aware, because our 'classical' expectations have been disrupted, of a foreign presence. This is the presence of an authoritative, narratorial agency, revealing a slant that not only contributes to the nature of the story, but also provides enunciatory sites from which we might infer film authorship.
>
> *Johnson, 1993, p. 56*

editing in psycho

If there's one thing that *Psycho* is famous for above all else it has to be the audaciously edited shower sequence. What makes the style of this short sequence so shocking is the way that it contrasts so violently with the rest of the film, and with the editing norms of conventional Hollywood cinema.

Throughout most of *Psycho* Alfred Hitchcock uses standard **continuity editing** techniques. When Marion and Norman take supper together, the dialogue is broken down into a shot/reverse shot sequence. Likewise, Alfred Hitchcock uses the standard editing grammar of establishing shots and eyeline-matches to create the spatial geography of the film's **diegetic world** and the punctuation marks of fades and dissolves to signify the end of scenes. And when Hitchcock wants to create suspense for the spectator he uses the established technique of **parallel editing** popular since the days of D.W. Griffith, to show Lila stuck in the Bates house while Norman knocks Sam out and comes after her.

The murder in the shower scene was different though, and Alfred Hitchcock knew that if he wanted to create a horrific murder that would get past the censors, he would have to innovate. To do this he turned back to the work of the Soviet film-makers of the 1920s who had experimented with montage.

To explain briefly, Soviet film-makers like Sergei Eisenstein embraced the new medium of cinema in the early years after the Russian revolution and attempted to create films that would communicate the glory of the revolution to the masses. Sergei Eisenstein believed the power of cinema lay in editing, or montage as the Soviets called it, and composed his own system of film-making based around the length, rhythm, graphic qualities and intellectual properties of individual shots – which only created meaning once they were edited together into a sequence.

Alfred Hitchcock applied similar principles to the construction of the murder in the shower. He could not actually show the murder, so what he did was create the effect of the murder through editing – and he was so successful that to this day many people believe that they see the knife going into Janet Leigh. Even when you know that you don't, the scene loses none of its power.

'It took us seven days to shoot that scene, and there were seventy camera setups for forty-five seconds of footage,' Alfred Hitchcock told François Truffaut (Truffaut, 1985, p. 277). The actual murder of Marion, from the time the shower curtain is pulled back to the moment when 'Mother' leaves the bathroom lasts for only twenty-two seconds, yet Alfred Hitchcock used over thirty shots. The extreme close-ups of Marion's face and mouth reveal her terror, while the shots showing the movement of the blade from screen top to bottom, alternated with shots of Marion's body, creates a momentum that gives the effect of the blade entering the body. Likewise, the rhythm of the cutting of the film mirrors the rhythm of the stabbing of the knife so that each film cut symbolically represents a cut to the body. Either side of the stabbing frenzy the montage creates two different effects. When Marion first steps into the shower the camera cuts between evenly paced shots of her, the shower head and the water that is gushing over her, cleansing her of the sins she has decided to absolve herself of by returning home. After the murder the frantic pace of the editing slows a little as Marion gradually sinks dead into the bath. Now the only movement in the shots is created by the flowing water that washes her life and blood away down the drain.

The editing in the shower sequence created one of the most frightening and famous scenes in film history. It demonstrates both Alfred Hitchcock's control over the techniques of his art and the power of cinema to create a shock effect for a mass audience.

psycho's sound

Film sound is one of the most underrated and neglected areas of film studies. Critics and theorists alike lavish attention on the stylistic merits of mise-en-scène, cinematography and editing, perhaps because the moving image is what gives cinema its uniqueness as a medium, but also perhaps because being able to understand and critically analyse music is a very specialised skill. However, nowhere is the importance of film sound demonstrated more clearly than in *Psycho*.

'strings alone'

Dialogue is one very important aspect of a film's soundtrack. The dialogue of *Psycho* is certainly crucial to the spectator's reading of the film as it is through this that one gathers plot information and learns much about the character's motivations, for example Marion's motivation to steal the money is explained by her conversation with Sam at the start of the film, and Norman's motivation to kill is partly explained when he tells Marion that a boy's best friend is his mother.

However, dialogue should not be over-analysed at the expense of other aspects of the soundtrack. If one takes away *Psycho*'s musical score, written by Bernard Herrmann, then one takes away much of the film's power over spectators. In an article on Bernard Herrmann's music Page Cook describes some of the functions served by *Psycho*'s musical score:

> The prologue opens with two startling stabs from the double bass, a perfect intimation of the jolting nature of the film to come. A kind of 'concerto' follows and brilliantly *probes* the psyches of the film's psychologically tormented characters. A minor key melody then weaves in and out of grimly syncopated tempi (celli and basses). This music is expanded more subtly for the scenes of Marion Crane's car ride to the Bates motel. For Marion's murder Herrmann uses high, sustained shrieks which sound bird-like.
>
> Cook, 1967, p. 409

Fred Steiner has analysed the musical score of *Psycho* in even greater detail. He asks,

> What is there about the *Psycho* music that sets it apart from other motion picture scores produced up to that time? The most noticeable departure from film music custom, and the one that concerns us here, is that Herrmann elected a daring and controversial orchestral combination: strings alone.
>
> Steiner, 1974, p. 31

Later in the article Fred Steiner reveals:

psycho's sound

> In a 1971 interview, [Herrmann] explained that he used only strings for *Psycho* because 'I felt that I was able to complement the black and white photography of the film with a black and white sound.'
>
> *Steiner, 1974, p. 32*

If one plays the whole sequence from Marion bidding Norman goodnight through to the murder, then one realises just how important the soundtrack is for cueing the expectations of spectators, building suspense and creating terror. As soon as Marion leaves Norman's office, Bernard Herrmann's score is faded in. It plays quietly with a slow tempo at first but the timbre of the music creates an uneasy feeling. As Norman removes the painting from the spyhole in his office the music moves up an octave and increases in volume. Norman then returns to the house, and as he does so the music subsides slightly and resumes a calmer timbre, perhaps reflecting Norman's attempt to subdue his desires. The film cuts back to Marion and as she flushes the calculations of the stolen money she has spent down the toilet and turns the shower on, the music is faded out, replaced only by the sound of the running water.

Originally Alfred Hitchcock was not going to use music for the shower murder scene. However, Bernard Herrmann persuaded him otherwise and the shrieking crescendo of violins played at a piercing volume and pitch provides the perfect aural counterpoint to the glinting cold knife that appears to be plunging into the body of Marion.

After Marion's death there is silence, apart from the sound of the running water. The music is then brought back in to underscore Norman's clean-up, building tension once again as the spectator wonders what is going to happen next.

Throughout the film the music score works subtly to build tension and suspense for the spectator. When the greatest moments of shock occur in the film: Marion and Arbogast's murders and Lila's discovery of Mrs Bates, the same screeching effect is brought in quickly and loudly to give emotional impact to the images on screen.

It is not just the music that contributes to the spectator's experience of the soundtrack. Sound effects are also extremely important. An anecdote about Alfred Hitchcock's choice of sound effect for Marion's stabbing illustrates this perfectly:

> Hitchcock developed a fascination for an aural technique to convey the sound a knife makes when jabbing a body. 'He told the prop man [Robert Bone] to go out and get a watermelon which we'd stab', recalled Marshal Schlom. 'Knowing Hitchcock, the prop man knew he had to come back not only with watermelons of all sizes, but casabas, cantaloupes, and honeydews.' (...) In a recording studio, prop man Bone auditioned the melons for Hitchcock, who sat listening with his eyes closed. When the demonstration table was littered with shredded fruit, Hitchcock opened his eyes, and intoned simply: 'Casaba.' The director was satisfied that he and his collaborators had married the precise sound and image for a stylised murder.
>
> *Rebello, 1998, p. 118*

conclusion

Psycho is a film full of stylistic innovations. From its string score and montage editing through to its voyeuristic cinematography and rich thematic mise-en-scène it is a film that can be read on many different levels by spectators.

However, in one sense Alfred Hitchcock wasn't innovating at all, what he was doing was reclaiming cinema from the stylistic grip of Classical Hollywood Narrative conventions. When sound came to the cinema in the late 1920s, film-makers abandoned many of the expressive film-making techniques of the silent era in favour of dialogue. However, Alfred Hitchcock's roots in the silent cinema meant he had the ability to utilise the entire stylistic cinematic repertoire. One part, right at the centre of *Psycho*, illustrates this perfectly. The sixteen-minute sequence, which runs from the time when Marion retires for the night through to the moment when her car sinks into the swamp, includes only one line of dialogue when Norman calls out to Mother about blood.

conclusion

a masterpiece of visual and aural film style

The rest of this sequence is told entirely through mise-en-scène, cinematography, sound and editing – and without the benefit of the inter-titles that the silent directors had. 'They were aroused by pure film,' Alfred Hitchcock said proudly of the effect his film had on spectators. He also claimed that, '*Psycho*, more than any of my other pictures, is a film that belongs to film-makers, to you and me' (Truffaut, 1985, p. 283).

Psycho is a masterpiece of visual and aural film style and it rightly deserves the plaudits that hail it as one of the greatest films ever made.

contexts

There is no right or wrong way to read a film. Each person will create their own unique reading based on their knowledge, personal experience and cultural background. Some spectators of *Psycho* will simply enjoy the effects of suspense and surprise within the film, while others with more specialist knowledge may gain pleasure from noting stylistic or thematic effects (see Narrative & Form and Style).

The reading of a film will of course change over time. Films do not exist in a void. Each film is shaped by the historical, political, social, and cultural context in which it is produced. There is no way that a modern spectator can experience *Psycho* in the same way as a spectator did in 1960. Although Gus Van Sant could recreate *Psycho*'s shots on celluloid in his 1998 remake, he could not recreate the shock of showing a naked **star** murdered in the shower or a toilet flushing on screen for the first time. Modern audiences are so used to seeing screen nudity and violence that much of *Psycho* really does seem tame when seen today.

historical and political context

Psycho opened in a boom time for America. Employment was high and the average person's standard of living was improving as modern domestic appliances, television sets and cars became more commonplace. In 1960 John F. Kennedy was running for president; Doris Day, Rock Hudson, Elizabeth Taylor and Debbie Reynolds were the box-office favourites and families enjoyed watching *I Love Lucy* and *The Flintstones* on television.

However, a great deal of social unrest bubbled beneath America's preferred 'Mom and apple pie' image of domestic harmony. Racial segregation of blacks and whites was still rife in the South and the Civil

social morality was changing

Rights movement, under the leadership of Martin Luther King, was gaining momentum. On an international level, the Cold War was escalating. The 1950s had seen American involvement in the Korean War and the McCarthy witchhunts which attempted to unmask communist sympathisers. In the early 1960s, just after *Psycho*'s release, things only got worse, with the Cuban missiles crisis of 1962 and the dispatch of American troops to Vietnam in 1963.

However, it wasn't just the politics of race and communism that were causing concern for American society. Social morality was also changing. The 1950s saw the rise of the teenager, rock and roll music and changing attitudes to sex outside marriage. As ridiculous as it might seem now, the fact that one American TV station would film the young Elvis Presley only from the waist up because it disapproved of his gyrating pelvis, shows just how much of a social threat youthful sexuality was perceived to be.

Alfred Hitchcock was well aware of the way in which his audience was changing. In cinema's heyday of the 1940s the audience was made up of a wide range of age groups. However, by the late 1950s families were staying at home to watch television more and more and therefore the demographic of cinema audiences was becoming predominantly younger. Describing his reasons for opening *Psycho* with the scene showing Marion in a brassiere after she has obviously just had sex with Sam, Alfred Hitchcock said:

> one of the reasons for which I wanted to do the scene in that way was that the audiences are changing. It seems to me that the straightforward kissing scene would be looked down at by the younger viewers; they'd feel it was silly. I know that they themselves behave as John Gavin and Janet Leigh did. I think that nowadays you have to show them the way they themselves behave most of the time.

Truffaut, 1985, p. 268

censorship

Alfred Hitchcock certainly took risks with his portrayal of sex, nudity and violence, and he knew that he would have to do battle with the censors to achieve the shocking results he had planned. In 1959 all films released in the United States had to adhere to the Production Code administered by the Motion Pictures Producers and Distributors of America (MPPDA). When the script was submitted to the Production Code office prior to shooting, Alfred Hitchcock was warned that it might be, 'impossible to issue a certificate on a finished film based on this script':

> Aside from the standard complaints by the Code office about dialogue peppered with uses of 'damn', 'God', and 'hell', the censorship board expressed deeper, more substantive reservations. The censors red-penciled a line of dialogue to be spoken to the heroine by Cassidy, the Texas oilman: 'Bed? Only playground that beats Las Vegas.' But more serious were charges that the Stefano script was shot through with '[a] very pointed description of an incestuous relationship between Norman and his mother' (...) It was also suggested that 'the discussion of transvestitism ... be eliminated.'
>
> Rebello, 1998, p. 77

The submission of scripts before shooting, and the subsequent guidance given by the Production Code office meant that film-makers in Hollywood generally worked within a framework of self-censorship: they knew what they could get away with and made their films accordingly. No film-maker wanted to make a film that would have to be severely cut, or worse still be refused certification, because of the enormous costs involved in making a film.

When Alfred Hitchcock submitted the finished *Psycho* to the Production Code office he was armed with a strategy to beat any complaints the censors might have. Janet Leigh recalled:

> He told me how he had planned all along to manipulate the censors by deliberately putting in things so bizarre, he could

come back to them and say, 'Tsk-tsk. All right, I'll take *that* out,
but you've got to give me this! He bargained with them like the
master he was.

Rebello, 1998, p. 145

One thing the censors did not like was the suggestion of nudity in the
shower scene. Apparently, three censors thought they saw nudity and
two did not. Alfred Hitchcock was asked to cut the offending shots, but
he didn't, he just sent the film back in. This time the censors who thought
they had seen nudity said it had gone, and the ones who hadn't seen
anything the first time thought they could see shots with nudity. Finally
Psycho was passed with just a few minor cuts to the dialogue.

When *Psycho* was released in Britain, the British Board of Film
Classification gave it an X certificate but required a shot of Anthony
Perkins looking at his bloodstained hands in the bathroom to be removed
and six frames of the stabbing of Arbogast to be cut.

ideological representations

Psycho's challenge to the censors certainly helped to push back the
boundaries of what was acceptable in the cinema at the start of the more
liberal era of the 1960s. However, from a film studies point of view, it is
interesting to note that it is not just social attitudes towards sex and
violence that have changed over the years. An analysis of *Psycho* also
reveals key facets of the **ideology** (i.e. the social ideas) of American
society at the end of the 1950s and beginning of the 1960s.

RACE

An analysis of the politics of *Psycho*'s **representation** of race is revealing
by virtue of its absence. Despite the multicultural ethnic mix of the
American population in 1959, the only characters shown on screen are
white. This was in line with virtually all Hollywood films of the period.
There were very few black actors working in Hollywood at all, and parts
for those black actors that did appear in films, such as Sidney Poitier,

Alfred Hitchcock's portrayal of nudity
and screen violence caused problems for
the censors, but helped push back the
boundaries of what was acceptable in the
cinema of the 1960s

were limited. Black actors usually appeared only in films that dealt with issues of race, and therefore where their colour was a central issue. Black actors were not seen in everyday roles, or as a film's main **protagonist**. The effect of this kind of representation was to reinforce the idea that America was a 'white' nation and that ethnic minorities were not accepted at the heart of society by virtue of the colour of their skin.

The problem of the racism implicit in the ideology of the films made at this time was compounded by the fact that there were virtually no black people employed in positions of power within the film industry. Gradually, over the past forty years, things have started to change and there are now more black and Asian actors and film-makers working in the cinema (although racism as a problem in the cinema is far from being resolved entirely).

SEX AND GENDER

Much has been written about the representation of gender and sexuality in *Psycho*. Marion's sexual behaviour is drawn attention to from the very beginning of the film. Once the camera has crept like a peeping Tom into the window of the motel room she is sharing with Sam, it comes to rest on Marion. She is lying on the bed wearing a bra. We have already been told that it is 2.43 in the afternoon on a Friday, and Marion confirms that they have had an illicit sexual liaison in a cheap motel when she says that hotels of this sort are interested in you only when your time is up.

The fact that Marion and Sam's relationship is outside the bounds of social acceptability is further reinforced when the conversation turns to a family dinner. Marion wants to meet Sam 'respectably', at her house, over dinner with her sister. But then Sam reminds her of the sexual nature of their relationship by suggesting that after dinner they send her sister to the movies and turn her mother's picture to the wall.

Because Marion and Sam are sleeping together outside marriage they are judged to have transgressed the moral code of the family. This point is further reinforced later in the film when Lila and Sam, who aren't involved in a sexual relationship, are accepted socially. They join the sheriff and his wife at church and are then invited for dinner. The threat

Marion's punishment for her overt sexuality

sexuality poses to the family is also voiced by 'Mrs Bates' when she hears that Norman has invited Marion in for supper and she makes it clear that Marion will not be satisfying her 'ugly appetite' with Norman.

The attitude towards unmarried sex in *Psycho* can be related to the prevalent social ideology of the day. As new contraceptive methods such as the pill were being introduced, young people's attitudes towards sex were changing and promiscuity was increasing. However, this shift in social attitude was creating tension because it threatened the basis of the family, where sex traditionally served the procreative process. Women who were sexually active outside marriage were seen as a particular threat because they might end up as unmarried mothers, and thus they were labelled by society as loose and morally reprehensible. *Psycho* reinforces this ideology because it is Marion who wants to have a 'respectable' family dinner and get married, whereas Sam seems more at ease with their situation.

However, before Marion can gain the respectability she craves, she is brutally murdered. Many critics have read the murder as a sign of Marion's punishment for her overt sexuality. Not only is she engaged in a sexual relationship outside marriage, but her visual appearance is coded as extremely sexual. She is seen in her brassiere and slip twice and all of her clothes are figure-hugging, particularly if one compares her costume with that of her more dowdy sister, Lila, who wears a smart suit and a loose-fitting coat throughout the film. Norman's comment to Marion that she eats like a bird can also be read as an aspersion about her sexuality. Norman implies that although Marion may try to appear dainty just like a bird she must really have a tremendous appetite and therefore, underneath the surface be a voracious man-eater.

When Marion takes a shower at the Bates Motel she is metaphorically cleansing away her sins because she has already decided to return home with the money. However, some critics have noted that as the camera cuts between shots of the gushing water and Marion's ecstatic face, the connotations are also of sexual enjoyment. The stabbing that follows can be read as a severe punishment for her sexual transgressions. It has also

ideological ...

been read as a symbolic rape by the penetrative knife, which takes on the form of the **phallus** for the sexually deviant Norman.

The violent murder of Marion (motivated by her sexuality rather than by her snooping – as Arbogast's murder and the attempted murder of Lila are) reveals not only society's attitudes to sex but also its attitudes to gender. Sam is not punished for his sexual behaviour but Marion is.

Feminist critics who have analysed *Psycho* see this as evidence both of Alfred Hitchcock's misogyny (because so many of his female characters die violent deaths) and of the more pervasive **patriarchal** ideology of Hollywood. Feminist criticism, based on the psychoanalytical theories of Sigmund **Freud**, and starting with the work of Laura Mulvey in the 1970s, analysed how Hollywood films – made almost exclusively by men – coded female stars as passive objects to be looked at as spectacle (coded through choice of actresses, lighting techniques, costume and make-up which all worked to accentuate an actress's beauty). However, according to Laura Mulvey, once actresses are made into spectacle, the spectator is confronted with the fact that women are different to men (i.e. they have no phallus) and therefore castration anxiety is evoked. (Castration anxiety is a central tenet of Sigmund Freud's psychoanalysis.) The result for female stars, according to Laura Mulvey, is that their threat has to be contained or destroyed. If one applies this theoretical approach to *Psycho* then Marion's violent death can be read as the patriarchal Hollywood system's extreme reaction to the threat of femininity at a time when women were being freed from the constraints of childbirth by new methods of contraception, and were thus taking on a more active role – both sexually and in terms of employment – within society.

A feminist approach provides one way in which the ideological representation of gender within *Psycho* can be read. Another critic, Tania Modleski, has considered the complexity of the representation of women in Alfred Hitchcock's films, which are 'always in danger of being subverted by females whose power is both fascinating and seemingly limitless' (Modleski, 1988, p. 1). If one takes this alternative approach then one can say that while Marion is certainly violently killed off in

links to other Hitchcock films

Psycho, she does form a strong and active presence as the protagonist in the first half of the film. She is then replaced by her virtual double, Lila, who is the one character who drives forward the search for Marion and then Arbogast and finally discovers the truth about Mrs Bates. Therefore the representation of female characters in *Psycho* is not all negative.

Analysing the representation of gender and sexuality in *Psycho* is a complex task. The fact that multiple readings can sit alongside each other demonstrates that every film contains many textual levels and that the reading of a film resides as much with the person doing the reading as it does with the way in which the film was created. As Tania Modleski says, '[Feminist] critics implicitly challenge and decenter directorial authority by considering Hitchcock's work as the expression of cultural attitudes and practices existing to some extent outside of the artist's control' (Modleski, 1988, p. 3). *Psycho*, therefore, is more than a product of Alfred Hitchcock's imaginative exploration of film-making techniques. It also contains, within its form, many of the ideas about gender and sexuality that were prevalent in society at the time it was produced.

cultural context

Just as *Psycho* can be related to the broader historical, social and political context in which it was made, so too the film needs to be placed within its cultural context. By understanding the relationship between *Psycho* and other films, one can further understand how the film creates meaning for its spectators.

Many of the ways in which *Psycho* relates to Alfred Hitchcock's other films have already been discussed. The recurrence of the theme of **voyeurism** can be traced backwards to Hitchcock films such as *Vertigo* and *Rear Window*, while the stylistic use of birds as a motif within the **mise-en-scène** has an obvious descendant in Alfred Hitchcock's later film *The Birds*. An analytical reading of *Psycho* as a Hitchcock film using the **auteur** approach is extremely fruitful because of the many obvious stylistic and thematic links to other Hitchcock films that can be made

'the first "modern" horror film'

(see Background: Hitchcock and the Auteur Theory). However, in many ways *Psycho* was radically different from other Hitchcock films, mainly because of its use of many of the conventions of the horror film, which was a new **genre** for Alfred Hitchcock. *Psycho* thus also needs to be considered within the context of the horror genre.

On a basic level, genre describes the way in which a film can be classified according to its visual motifs, character types and narrative structure; for example, films are usually classified as horror if they contain images of dark creepy houses, are populated with supernatural characters and have a narrative structure that revolves around the fight between good and evil. Genres provide a framework for a spectator's reading of a film because they define the spectator's expectations of what will happen. However, films can't just repeat the same basic pattern. Each film must also provide a variation on the genre that will make it unique. Therefore genres are constantly evolving with each new addition.

When Alfred Hitchcock made *Psycho* he deliberately turned his attention to the low-budget horror films he had noticed were popular with audiences at the time and were thus making money. Alfred Hitchcock wanted to know what would happen if an established director, such as himself, made a horror film with the bigger budget and stars that he could attract. He never quite had this question answered though, because Paramount refused to back the film (see Background: The Production of *Psycho*) and therefore the director had to provide his own finance and forgo the usual high production values and big stars he was used to. Although Alfred Hitchcock wanted to make a horror film, he also decided to innovate with many of the conventions of the established horror genre. Therefore, *Psycho* was not an average horror movie.

> Alfred Hitchcock's *Psycho* has been hailed as the first 'modern' horror film. The reasons given in support of this claim are usually thematic – in *Psycho*, the 'monster' is not some unnatural, unholy creation, as 'other' who stands utterly outside our existing conceptual scheme. Rather, the monster here is human, all too human, and besides that, all too real (...) After *Psycho*, emotionally traumatised and psychosexually motivated monster-

> murderers began appearing in horror films with alarming
> regularity.
>
> *Schneider, 1999, p. 70*

Not only is *Psycho* credited with being the first modern horror film, it is
also defined as the mother of the 'slasher' sub-genre within the genre of
horror. Carol J. Clover explains why:

> The appointed ancestor of the slasher film is Hitchcock's *Psycho*.
> Its elements are familiar: the killer is the psychotic product of a
> sick family, but still recognisably human; the victim is a beautiful,
> sexually active woman; the location is not-home, at a Terrible
> Place; the weapon is something other than a gun; the attack is
> registered from the victim's point of view and comes with
> shocking suddenness. None of these features is original, but the
> unprecedented success of Hitchcock's particular formulation,
> above all the sexualisation of both motive and action, prompted
> a flood of imitations and variations.
>
> *Clover, 1992, p. 23-4*

Those imitations and variations include films such as *The Texas Chainsaw
Massacre* (1974), *Halloween* (1978) and the *Friday The 13th* (1980) and
Nightmare on Elm Street films, as well as *Psycho*'s own three sequels
(none of which was directed by Alfred Hitchcock).

> The spiritual debt of all the post-1974 slasher films to *Psycho*
> is clear, and it is a rare example that does not pay a visual
> tribute, however brief, to the ancestor – if not in a shower
> stabbing, then in a purling drain or the shadow of a knife-
> wielding hand.
>
> *Clover, 1992, p. 26*

Most genres revolve in cycles of popularity, and the slasher genre has
resurfaced in a new form in the late 1990s and early 2000, with films
such as *I Know What You Did Last Summer* (1997) and the *Scream* trilogy
of genre parodies (1996, 1997 and 2000).

defies easy genre categorisation

However, although *Psycho* may well have spawned its own sub-genre, it defies easy genre categorisation itself, and this is what makes the film particularly complex for a spectator to read. Much of *Psycho*'s **iconography** certainly relates to the horror genre, for example the dark Gothic mansion, which hides a terrible secret in its cellar, fleeting glimpses of an 'undead monster' in the form of Mother, the blood of the murders and the stabbing knife. The film's structure around the suspense and shock of the murders can also be related to the horror genre. However, Alfred Hitchcock grafts other generic structures on top of the horror conventions. R. Barton Palmer identifies a generic strand of melodrama at the start of the film when the focus is on Marion's relationship with Sam, which then gives way to elements from the horror genre, the detective genre and **film noir**. The interweaving of these different generic strands creates problems for the film's **closure** (see Narrative & Form: Alternative Narrative Structure) because, as R. Barton Palmer says, 'Hitchcock's irony effectively places characters and viewers in different genres, the ones in search of an answer to a mysterious disappearance, the others eager for an explanation of a terrifying presence' (Barton Palmer, 1986, p. 17).

To add to the list of genres that can be identified in *Psycho*, the film is often labelled a thriller, a genre in which Alfred Hitchcock worked extensively. The director also claimed that the film was a fun picture and a black comedy, much to the concern of contemporary critics, who thought his macabre vision was already twisted enough. '*Psycho* is a film that was made with quite a sense of amusement on my part. To me it's a fun picture ... It's rather like taking [the audience] through the haunted house at the fairground or the roller-coaster' (Rebello, 1998, p. 168). While one can perhaps see the humour in Norman Bates's bizarre appearance dressed as Mother at the end of the film, and appreciate the tongue-in-cheek comments such as, 'Mother isn't quite herself today', the horror of Norman Bates somehow always manages to take the edge off of the 'jokes'. Perhaps Alfred Hitchcock's claims for comedy had more to do with his attempt to fuel his public persona as a prankster and his need to deflect some of the unnerving horror he had evidently unleashed with *Psycho*.

cultural influence

There can be no doubt that *Psycho* has had a huge influence on Western culture. It is far easier to name the films under its influence, from *The Texas Chainsaw Massacre* through to *Scream*, than it is to identify the films that influenced *Psycho* – although there were some, such as Fritz Lang's *M* (1931) and Henri-Georges Clouzot's *Les Diaboliques* (1954). *Psycho* is much more a *source* than a *site* of **intertextual** stylistic and generic references, and this is what made the film so original – and partly explains why it had the impact on audiences at the time of its release that it did.

Evidence that *Psycho* is a key text in our culture can be found on the Internet Movie Database (www.imdb.com). For every film listed on the site there are usually links to a few other films that make reference to that film. For *Psycho* the list stretches to ninety films, including *The Haunting* (1963), *Halloween*, *Raging Bull* (1980), *Pulp Fiction* (1994), *Bride of Chucky* (1998) and *American Psycho* (2000), and more than thirty other films that spoof *Psycho* in one way or another. Stephen Rebello cites even more cultural references:

> In *Carrie* (1976), director Brian De Palma named the high school attended by the heroine 'Bates High School'. Hitchcock's film has spawned Bates Motel T-shirts and shower curtains. The shower scene has been parodied by such filmmakers as Mel Brooks in *High Anxiety* [1977] and reworked by Brian De Palma in *Dressed to Kill* [1980] and by Roman Polanski in *Frantic* (1988).
>
> *Rebello, 1998, p. 189*

Stephen Rebello goes on to say that Adrian Lyne 'was acutely aware of the shadow of Hitchcock looming over *Fatal Attraction* [1987]' (Rebello, 1998, p. 193).

Intertextual references also extend to films that may not make direct reference to *Psycho* but that rework elements of *Psycho*'s textual system. Julie Tharp is one critic who has analysed how *The Silence of the Lambs* (1990) draws on *Psycho*. Buffalo Bill, the murderer with a skin fetish in

cultural influence

The Silence of the Lambs, is based on the same real-life serial killer, Ed Gein, who was the inspiration for the character of Norman Bates (see Background: The Production of *Psycho*). However, Julie Tharp argues that the intertextual references flow much deeper:

> In addition to the 'transvestite' murderers, Lila *Crane* is doubled by Clarice *Starling*; the psychologist in *Psycho* is expanded in the character of Dr. Frederick Chilton; Sheriff Chambers gets a slick, though still paternalist, makeover in Jack Crawford (...); and perhaps the most grim transformation is that of Sam Loomis – male protagonist and Lila's helpmate – to Anthony Hopkins' Hannibal Lecter, Starling's mentor.
>
> *Tharp, 1991, pp. 107–8*

Another critic who has looked at the way *Psycho* has been reworked in a later text is Rod S. Heimpel. He begins his work by providing a useful definition of intertextuality:

> Theories of intertextuality and source-influence both admit that all texts derive their meaning (and their ability to mean) from other texts. A text's *intertextual identity* depends on both its source-influences and also on the texts which it carefully incorporates and transforms.
>
> *Heimpel, 1994, p. 46*

He then goes on to analyse how Stephen Frear's *The Grifters* (1990) works through elements of the narrative structure, character types and iconography of *Psycho*.

> The closest narrative relation between Hitchcock's and Frear's films is provided by the chase scenes where in each case a woman ends up at a desolate roadside motel where she is murdered/assailed during the first night of her stay. (...) the brief sequence depicting Lilly turning off the main road and driving up to a motel outside of Phoenix tends to *re-call* the now iconographic image of Marion driving up to a motel fifteen miles

an early precursor of postmodernism in the cinema

> outside of Fairvale: darkness, winding roads, suspenseful music,
> and finally, a looming neon 'MOTEL' sign.
>
> *Heimpel, 1994, p. 54*

The way in which *Psycho* has fed into so many other film texts in the last forty years shows how all films need to be placed within their cultural context. The cultural knowledge an audience brings to a film keeps on expanding in an ever increasing circle, and as general cultural knowledge has expanded, so all kinds of cultural texts, from novels to paintings to films have explored their relationship with their own cultural heritage in a self-aware **postmodern** style.

Released in 1960, *Psycho* can perhaps be seen as an early precursor of postmodernism in the cinema, both in the way it draws attention to its own formal construction as a text with its consideration of voyeurism (see Narrative & Form: Narrative Structure and Hitchcock as Auteur, and Style: *Psycho*'s Mise-en-scène and *Psycho*'s Cinematography) and also in the way it fused the boundaries between high art and low art.

Throughout its early history cinema was regarded as one of the low arts, mainly because of its popular status with a mass audience (which was largely working class). This meant the cinema could not possibly be regarded with the same seriousness as the high arts of the classic novel, opera or the theatre. However, in the 1950s, a group of French intellectual critics started to reappraise the films of some Hollywood film-makers, Alfred Hitchcock among them, as works that carried the authorial signature of a great artist, with the camera working as their 'palette' (see Background: Hitchcock and the Auteur Theory).

With *Psycho*, Alfred Hitchcock pushed his acceptance as an 'artist' to the limit. The horror genre was already considered one of the lowest genres within the hierarchy of cinema, still largely regarded as a low art. 'Even within film itself, which is necessarily a lower-class form in relation to "high culture", there are hierarchic divisions traced along genre lines: suspense films are classier than horror films, romantic comedies classier than slapstick' (Paul, 1994, p. 32). And yet, within that genre, Alfred Hitchcock managed to achieve something great. Few critics realised it at the time – although *Sight and Sound* was one magazine that published a positive review in 1960, '*Psycho* comes nearer to attaining an exhilarating balance between content and style than anything Hitchcock has done in years' (Autumn 1960, p. 19). But within a few years *Psycho* was being hailed as a masterpiece of the cinema. In 1960 Bosley Crowther of *The New York Times* called *Psycho*, 'a blot on an honorable career', and yet in 1965, he praised Roman Polanski's film *Repulsion* as, 'a psychological thriller in the classic style of *Psycho*' (Rebello, 1998, p. 165).

Psycho's acceptance both by the mass public as a hugely popular film, and, eventually, by the critical establishment as a 'classic work of art', demonstrates how the boundaries between high 'art' and popular culture were shifting in the postmodern era of the late twentieth century. *Psycho* can thus be considered as a key text in the cultural history of the century.

PSYCHO'S INFLUENCE ON THE FILM INDUSTRY

Psycho's influence on our cinematic heritage is undoubted, but its influence extends not just to the end product of films. *Psycho* also had a tremendous impact on the process of film-making, film **distribution** and film **exhibition** in Hollywood.

Throughout his career in Hollywood, Alfred Hitchcock worked under contract to various **studios**. This was the norm in the era of the **studio system**, where the studios organised their business around a system of **vertical integration**. This meant the studios had control over every aspect of a film's life: a film was made on the sound stages owned by the studio by employees under contract to the studio; it was then promoted by the studio's own publicity department and distributed to cinemas owned by each studio. This system effectively kept out any competition from independent film-makers, particularly in America: if you didn't work for a studio then you had virtually no chance of getting a film made or seen by the public.

The American government eventually looked into the anti-competitive tactics of the Hollywood studios and in the 1950s brought **anti-trust legislation** against them, which broke up their monopoly. Most studios

devolved film-making could work

sold off their cinemas and production facilities and instead began to concentrate on financing and distributing films.

When Alfred Hitchcock wanted to make *Psycho* in 1959, the studio he was contracted to, Paramount, did not want to back the film because it felt it was unsuitable for the cinema (see Background: The Production of *Psycho*). However, Alfred Hitchcock decided to go ahead with the film in a manner that anticipated the way modern Hollywood would work. The director put up most of the money for the film's production and negotiated his own deal to use a Universal sound stage for filming. Paramount did agree to distribute the film though, which meant Alfred Hitchcock could rely on Paramount's power to publicise *Psycho*, and he was guaranteed that it would be shown in cinemas and thus stood a chance of recouping its production costs. The success of *Psycho* all over the world proved to Paramount and other studios that this newer system of devolved film-making could work. The way that *Psycho* was distributed and promoted also reveals something about the way Hollywood cinema was changing in 1959. The most famous trailer for the film, which is included on the most recent VHS and DVD releases of *Psycho*, had Alfred Hitchcock giving a tour of the Bates Motel and house. The director whets the audience's appetite for the film by divulging titbits of information; for example he says, 'The bathroom ... Well they've cleaned all this up now. Big difference. You should have seen the blood, the whole place was ... well it's too horrible to describe.'

The norm for theatrical trailers was to give short excerpts from a film to encourage audiences to see it. Alfred Hitchcock's method with *Psycho* was unusual because he did not allow audiences to see any action from the film, but by describing it to them he knew he was already building suspense and anticipation.

Psycho's theatrical trailer ends with a title stating, 'The picture you must see from the beginning... or not at all! ... for no one will be seated after the start of Alfred Hitchcock's greatest shocker, "Psycho".' Alfred Hitchcock's billing above the film's title was significant because he was one of the only directors at the time who was recognised as a 'star name'. Paramount knew that the fact that *Psycho* was a 'Hitchcock' film, meant

cultural influence

that it would sell to audiences. This marketing technique is still used today with films made by directors that the distributors know have loyal fans; for example *Casino* is tagged as a 'Martin Scorsese' film.

The trailer's reference to the fact that people would not be seated after the film had started caused uproar when the film was released in 1960 (see Background: The Impact of *Psycho*). Audiences were not used to attending a film at a set publicised time and thus *Psycho* challenged their viewing habits, setting off long queues at cinemas all around the world.

Psycho did not just alter audience's cinema-going habits though, it also gave audiences a very different experience once they were seated in the cinema, and this is probably what made the film such an international phenomenon.

Linda Williams is one critic who has commented on how *Psycho* affected audiences, and in turn how this affected the development of Hollywood cinema, and she is worth quoting at length:

> talk to anyone old enough to have seen *Psycho* on its release in a movie theatre and they will tell you what it felt like to be scared out of their wits. I vividly remember a Saturday matinee in 1960 when two girlfriends and I spent much of the screening with our eyes shut listening to the music and to the audience's screams as we tried to guess when we might venture to look again at a screen whose terrors were unaccountably thrilling.
>
> Most people who saw *Psycho* for the first time in a theatre have similarly vivid memories. Many will recall the shock of the shower murder and how they were afraid to take showers for months or years afterwards. But if it is popularly remembered that *Psycho* altered the bathing habits of a nation, it is less well recalled how it fundamentally changed viewing habits. (...)
>
> With *Psycho*, cinema in some ways reverted to what the critic Tom Gunning has described as the 'attractions' of pre-classical cinema – an experience that has more of the effect of a roller coaster ride than the absorption of a classical narrative.
>
> Anyone who has gone to the movies in the last twenty years

'the "visceral, kinetic" appeal of post-classical cinema'

cannot help but notice how entrenched this roller coaster sensibility of repeated tension and release, assault and escape has become. While narrative is not abandoned, it often takes second place to a succession of visual and auditory shocks and thrills which are, as Thomas Schatz puts it in 'The New Hollywood', 'visceral, kinetic and fast paced, increasingly reliant on special effects, increasingly "fantastic" ... and increasingly targeted at younger audiences.' Schatz cites *Jaws* (1975) as the precursor of the New Hollywood calculated blockbuster, but the film that set the stage for the 'visceral, kinetic' appeal of post-classical cinema was *Psycho*.

Williams, 1994, p. 15

conclusion

Psycho is one film that can genuinely claim to be a landmark in film history. Not only because it is one of the best-known films ever made, but also because of its legacy. It pushed back the boundaries of what was acceptable within the American cinema; provided audiences with a completely new kind of cinematic experience, which they loved even though they were terrified; and showed that even the most popular kind of mass entertainment could be considered an art worth taking seriously.

Psycho is therefore a key text in the work of film studies. Analysis of its mise-en-scène, **cinematography**, sound, editing and narrative demonstrates just how a film text creates meaning for its spectators; while analysis of the many critical readings of the film that exist (and many have been cited in this book) shows how the film relates to its historical, social, political, ideological and cultural context.

With *Psycho*, Alfred Hitchcock proved once and for all that he was not just the master of suspense, but also a master of the cinema. His influence, and that of *Psycho*, haunts the cinema like the ghost of Mrs Bates over Norman, reminding us that no film can escape the cultural heritage of its past.

Norman Bates and *Psycho*
have continued to haunt
the cinema for the past
forty years

bibliography

general film

Altman, Rick, *Film Genre,*
BFI, 1999
Detailed exploration of film genres

Bordwell, David, *Narration in the Fiction Film,* Routledge, 1985
A detailed study of narrative theory and structures

– – –, Staiger, Janet & Thompson, Kristin, *The Classical Hollywood Cinema: Film Style & Mode of Production to 1960,* Routledge, 1985; pbk 1995
An authoritative study of cinema as institution, it covers film style and production

– – – & Thompson, Kristin, *Film Art,* McGraw-Hill, 4th edn, 1993
An introduction to film aesthetics for the non-specialist

Branson, Gill & Stafford, Roy, *The Media Studies Handbook,* Routledge, 1996

Buckland, Warren, *Teach Yourself Film Studies,* Hodder & Stoughton, 1998
Very accessible, it gives an overview of key areas in film studies

Cook, Pam (ed.), *The Cinema Book,* BFI, 1994

Corrigan, Tim, *A Short Guide To Writing About Film,* HarperCollins, 1994
What it says: a practical guide for students

Dyer, Richard, *Stars,* BFI, 1979; pbk Indiana University Press, 1998
A good introduction to the star system

Easthope, Antony, *Classical Film Theory,* Longman, 1993
A clear overview of recent writing about film theory

Hayward, Susan, *Key Concepts in Cinema Studies,* Routledge, 1996

Hill, John & Gibson, Pamela Church (eds), *The Oxford Guide to Film Studies,* Oxford University Press, 1998
Wide-ranging standard guide

Lapsley, Robert & Westlake, Michael, *Film Theory: An Introduction,* Manchester University Press, 1994

Maltby, Richard & Craven, Ian, *Hollywood Cinema,* Blackwell, 1995
A comprehensive work on the Hollywood industry and its products

Mulvey, Laura, 'Visual Pleasure and Narrative Cinema' (1974), in *Visual and Other Pleasures,* Indiana University Press, Bloomington, 1989
The classic analysis of 'the look' and 'the male gaze' in Hollywood cinema. Also available in numerous other edited collections

Nelmes, Jill (ed.), *Introduction to Film Studies,* Routledge, 1996
Deals with several national cinemas and key concepts in film study

Nowell-Smith, Geoffrey (ed.), *The Oxford History of World Cinema,* Oxford University Press, 1996
Hugely detailed and wide-ranging with many features on 'stars'

PSYCHO

Thomson, David, *A Biographical Dictionary of the Cinema*, Secker & Warburg, 1975
Unashamedly driven by personal taste, but often stimulating

Truffaut, François, *Hitchcock*, Simon & Schuster, 1966, rev. edn. Touchstone, 1985
Landmark extended interview

Turner, Graeme, *Film as Social Practice*, 2nd edn, Routledge, 1993
Chapter four, 'Film Narrative', discusses structuralist theories of narrative

*Wollen, Peter, *Signs and Meaning in the Cinema*, Viking 1972
An important study in semiology

Readers should also explore the many relevant websites and journals. *Film Education* and *Sight and Sound* are standard reading.

Valuable websites include:

The Internet Movie Database at
http://uk.imdb.com

Screensite at
http://www.tcf.ua.edu/screensite/contents.html

The Media and Communications Site at the University of Aberystwyth at
http://www.aber.ac.uk/~dgc/welcome.html

There are obviously many other university and studio websites which are worth exploring in relation to film studies.

psycho

'*Psycho* and *The Apartment* review', *Sight and Sound*, vol. 29, no. 4, autumn 1960

Astruc, Alexandre, 'The birth of a new avant-garde: La caméra-stylo', in Peter Graham (ed.), *The New Wave: Critical Landmarks*, Secker and Warburg/BFI, 1968

Barton Palmer, R., 'The Experience of Viewing and the Viewing of Experience in *Rear Window* and *Psycho*', *Cinema Journal*, no. 2, winter 1986

Bass, Saul, 'The "Compleat Film Maker" – From Titles to Features', *American Cinematographer*, vol. 58, no. 3, March 1977

Bellour, Raymond, 'Psychosis, Neurosis, Perversion', *Camera Obscura: A Journal of Feminism and Film Theory*, no. 3-4, summer 1979

Bogdanovich, Peter, *The Cinema of Alfred Hitchcock*, The Museum of Modern Art, 1963

Clover, Carol J., *Men, Women and Chainsaws: Gender in the Modern Horror Film*, BFI, 1992

Cook, Page, 'Bernard Herrmann', *Films in Review*, vol. 18, no. 7, August-September 1967

Creed, Barbara, *The Monstrous-Feminine: Film, Feminism, Psychoanalysis*, Routledge, 1993

French, Philip, review in *The Observer*, 2 August 1998

Heimpel, Rod S., 'Hitchcock's *Psycho* in Stephen Frear's *The Grifters*', *Canadian Journal of Film Studies*, vol. 3, no. 1, spring 1994

Hesling, W.J.M., 'Classical Cinema and the Spectator', *Literature/Film Quarterly*, vol. 15, no. 3, 1987

James, Nick, quoted in an article by Paul McCann in *The Independent*, 6 August 1999

Johnson, Kenneth, 'The Point of View of the Wandering Camera', *Cinema Journal*, vol. 32, no. 2, winter 1993

Kirkham, Pat, 'The Jeweller's Eye', *Sight and Sound*, vol. 7, no. 4, April 1997

Leigh, Janet, '*Psycho*, Rosie and a Touch of Orson', *Sight and Sound*, vol. 39, no. 2, spring 1970

Leigh, Janet and Nickens, Christopher *Psycho: Behind the Scenes of the Classic Thriller*, Harmony Books, 1995

MacColl, Rene, review in the *Daily Express*, 2 July 1960

Modleski, Tania, *The Women Who Knew Too Much: Hitchcock and Feminist Theory*, Methuen, 1988

Norman, Barry, review in the *Daily Mail*, 8 August 1969

Paul, William, *Laughing Screaming: Modern Hollywood Horror and Comedy*, Columbia University Press, 1994

Rebello, Stephen, *Alfred Hitchcock and the Making of Psycho*, Marion Boyars, 1998

A detailed overview of the production of the film, including interviews with many key personnel

Schneider, Steven, 'Manufacturing Horror in Hitchcock's *Psycho*', *CineAction*, no. 50, September 1999

Schuman, Howard, article in *The Guardian*, 17 July 1998

Sloan, Jane E., *Alfred Hitchcock: The Definitive Filmography: A Guide to References and Resources*, University of California Press, 1993

Steiner, Fred, 'Herrmann's "Black and White" Music for Hitchcock's *Psycho*', *Film Music Notebook*, vol. 1, fall and winter 1974

Taylor, John Russell, *Hitch: The Life and Times of Alfred Hitchcock*, Da Capo Press, 1996

A detailed overview of Hitchcock's career

Tharp, Julie, 'The Transvestite as Monster: Gender Horror in *The Silence of the Lambs*', *Journal of Popular Film and Television*, vol. 19, no. 3, fall 1991

Walker, Alexander, review in the *Evening Standard*, 30 July 1998

Williams, Linda, 'Learning to Scream', *Sight and Sound*, vol. 4, no. 12, December 1994

Wood, Robin, *Hitchcock's Films Revisited*, Columbia University Press, 1989

An update of Wood's seminal work on Hitchcock as an auteur

www.paradiselost.org/psycho.html

An online version of the *Psycho* screenplay

www.afionline.org

The American Film Institute website

www.the-movie-times.com

A movie website that lists, among other things, the box-office takings of the most successful films

cinematic terms

180° rule an editing technique that maintains spatial continuity and screen direction. If the camera stays on the same side of an imaginary line drawn between the actors throughout a scene then the actors will remain consistently on one side of the image. However, if the camera crosses the line then an actor who was on the left of the screen will suddenly jump to the right-hand side of the screen, potentially disorientating the spectator

35° rule an editing technique. An edit needs to change the angle of the image by more than 35° for it to look like a 'proper' cut, which has been motivated by the need to change position. An edit of less than 35° looks like a jump cut

anti-trust legislation brought against the Hollywood studios by the US government in the 1950s in order to break the monopoly of film-making by the studios

auteur a term describing a film-maker who is considered to be an artist or the author of their films

B-movies films made cheaply by Hollywood studios to support the main feature films showing at the cinema

Cahiers du cinéma a French film journal that has published debates on film theory from the 1950s to the present

cause and effect a technique used in Classical Hollywood Narrative films, which means that every scene is linked and motivated. Nothing is included in the narrative that is not relevant, for example if a close-up of a teacup is shown then it means there is something wrong with the teacup, e.g. it is poisoned. At the end of each scene cues are given for the next, e.g. a character might say they need to investigate something and the next scene would show them in a library. What would not be shown would be their journey to the library

cinematography a term that describes everything related to the camera in filming: film stock, film speed, framing (i.e. the distance, level, height and angle of the camera) and camera movement

Classical Hollywood Narrative the system of narrative used in Hollywood films made between the 1930s and the 1950s. The Classical Hollywood Narrative system was made up of a number of narrative conventions that made films easy to follow for a mass audience

close-up denoting a short distance between the camera and subject/object filmed: a close-up of a person would show just one feature e.g. a face or hands

closure a Classical Hollywood Narrative term that describes how all the loose ends of a plot are tied up so that the narrative can be brought to a close

continuity editing the system of editing used in Classical Hollywood Narrative films. Continuity editing consists of a number of techniques that maintain spatial and temporal continuity even when a narrative moves between lots of locations or cuts out big chunks of time. Continuity editing techniques are usually motivated so that they are not noticed or disruptive. This enables the spectator to concentrate on the narrative

cinematic terms

cut an edit that simply splices two shots together

diegetic world the fictional world in which the characters of a narrative live

dissolve an edit whereby one image dissolves or mixes into the next

distribute/distribution the process by which films are booked into cinemas. The term also describes the way films are advertised and marketed to audiences

enunciation the process of narrating a story. Enunciation describes *how* a story is told

enunciator the narrator of a story. Often in the cinema the narrator or enunciator is not made obvious, i.e. there is not a voice-over from someone who appears to be telling the story. In a situation such as this the enunciator can be considered as the film-maker

equilibrium/disruption/re-equilibrium describes the pattern of storytelling in Classical Hollywood Narrative films. An equilibrium (i.e. a balance) exists at the start of a narrative, a disruption occurs, and the work of the narrative is to get to the point of re-equilibrium so that harmony can be re-established within the narrative world

establishing shot a continuity editing technique that requires each scene of a film to start with a long shot showing the location of the action and the relative positions of characters

exhibitor/exhibition the screening of films in cinemas, on video or on television. An exhibitor is an organisation that screens films

eyeline-match a continuity editing technique. An eyeline-match occurs when a close-up of an actor's face is followed with a shot of another person or object. Even though the subject/object are not physically in the frame together, the spectator makes a mental link and accepts that the actor in the first shot is looking at the person or object in the second shot. This creates a three-dimensional space for the film's action from two-dimensional images

fade an edit whereby the image either fades up from black or fades down to black. Normally signals the beginning or end of a scene

feminist critics a term used to describe critics and theorists who analyse the representation of gender in films and other cultural artefacts from a feminist perspective. Feminists critics are particularly interested in analysing the relationship between how women are portrayed in films and their position in society

film noir a term given by French critics to a genre of Hollywood films made between the 1940s and the 1950s. Film noirs were usually set in an urban criminal underworld. The visual style of film noirs was dark and shadowy. Critics believe film noirs reflected a sense of social disaffection related to the effects of the Second World War

Freud Sigmund Freud (1856–1939), Austrian neurologist who developed his own method and theory of psychoanalysis

genre a way of classifying a type of film e.g. as a western, a musical or a horror film. Each genre can be identified by visual, aural, narrative and thematic characteristics

cinematic terms

German Expressionism an avant-garde art movement in Germany in the 1910s and 1920s, which exaggerated and distorted the objects it depicted in order to reflect the angst of the artists. German Expressionism first appeared in the cinema with *The Cabinet of Dr Caligari* (1920)

high angle a term used to describe a camera shot taken from high up, looking down

iconography a term describing the visual motifs/objects associated with particular genres of film. For instance, the iconography of the gangster film consists of guns, cars, smart suits and cities

ideology the ideas, beliefs and norms of behaviour held by a society at a particular historical moment

intertextual the referencing of other artistic or cultural texts such as plays, novels, films, music or paintings within a text

long shot denoting a long distance between the camera and subject/object filmed: a long shot of a person would show the whole of their body and their background and location

low angle a term used to describe a camera shot taken from low down, looking up

match–on–action a continuity editing technique. A match-on-action is when an edit takes place in the middle of an action. For example, shot one might show a person sitting down while shot two shows them standing. The cut occurs during the movement from sitting to standing. This ensures that the edit goes unnoticed because the spectator is distracted by the act of movement itself

medium shot denoting a medium distance between the camera and subject/object filmed: a medium shot of a person would show their body from the waist up

mise-en-scène from the French term meaning 'put in to the scene'. Describes everything in the image that has been placed in front of the camera for filming: set design, location, costume, make-up, props, actors, acting style and lighting effects

overlapping sound a continuity editing technique that links scenes together. As one scene ends and the next begins any music playing in the first scene is carried over to the start of the next scene

pan a camera movement, where the camera head moves horizontally from side to side

parallel editing a style of editing developed in the early days of cinema, whereby a film cuts between two different pieces of action taking place simultaneously, for example cutting between the heroine tied to the railway track and the hero racing to save her. It is usually used to create suspense

patriarchal a term that describes a society where men hold the dominant positions of power

phallus a term used in psychoanalysis to describe the male penis

point of view a term used to describe a shot taken from a character's subjective position. The effect is that the spectator sees things as if through the eyes of the character

cinematic terms

politique des auteurs a manifesto published in *Cahiers du cinéma* in the early 1950s. The *politique des auteurs* called for the rejection of the traditional French 'cinema of quality' in favour of a cinema that would allow individual film-makers to express themselves as artists

postmodern a term used to define a style of art or culture that is self-aware and self-referential

protagonist the main character within a narrative, usually 'the hero'. Everything in a Classical Hollywood Narrative film revolves around the protagonist

representation a term that describes the cinematic presentation of ideological constructs such as gender, race, age, class and sexuality

screenplay can also be called a shooting script. A screenplay is produced from a script and includes instructions for the camera and the art department, as well as for the actors

shot/reverse shot a continuity editing technique used for dialogue scenes. First both of the actors engaged in a conversation are shown in a two-shot, then the camera cuts in to medium shots and close-ups of one actor and then the other, usually from a position 'over the shoulder' of the other actor. This pattern allows long dialogue scenes to be broken down, so that the spectator sees the significant facial expressions and reactions of the actors as they speak

stars term describing the leading actors and actresses in Hollywood films

star system describes the way a star's image is promoted in order to sell a film

storyboards a series of drawings made up from the screenplay or script of a film, depicting the action and camera position

studios the studios, e.g. Warner Brothers, MGM and Paramount, controlled the whole process of film production from the 1920s to the 1950s

studio system describes the way in which the studios organised the production, distribution and exhibition of their films

superimposed where one or more images are placed on top of each other, so that they can all be seen at once

tracking shot a camera movement where the camera is moved forwards, backwards or to the side

vertical integration a term that describes how the studios had control of every stage of film production, distribution and exhibition between the 1920s and the 1950s. The studios financed films, produced them in their own studios, publicised them and then screened them in the cinemas they owned. Vertical integration meant that the studios could monopolise film production

voice-over a sound technique where an actor voices thoughts over an image. The spectator of the film can hear the voice, but the other characters in the film cannot

voyeurism/voyeuristic a term used to describe the pleasurable act of watching someone, usually when they are not aware they are being watched

zoom a movement of the camera lens that resembles the movement of a camera tracking in or out

credits

production companies
Shamley Productions,
Paramount Pictures Corporation

director
Alfred Hitchcock

producer
Alfred Hitchcock

screenplay
Joseph Stefano

director of photography
John L. Russell

editor
George Tomasini

art directors
Joseph Hurley, Robert Clatworthy

music
Bernard Herrmann

titles designer/pictorial consultant
Saul Bass

assistant director
Hilton A. Green

original novel
Robert Bloch

cast
Norman Bates – Anthony Perkins
Marion Crane – Janet Leigh
Lila Crane – Vera Miles
Sam Loomis – John Gavin
Milton Arbogast – Martin Balsam
Sheriff Al Chambers – John McIntire
Mrs Chambers – Lurene Tuttle
Dr Richmond – Simon Oakland
Tom Cassidy – Frank Albertson
Caroline – Patricia Hitchcock
George Lowery – Vaughn Taylor
Car salesman – John Anderson
Policeman – Mort Mills